# GHOSTING

## MARC JOHNSON

First Edition, 2020

ISBN 978-0-98-34770-1-3

Longshot Publishing

# CHAPTER 1

**MAX STUFFED HIS** hands into the pockets of his old coat. It was a nervous habit he had developed in his youth. No matter how old he got or how many times he ventured to the club, he couldn't quite break that habit. What did he have to be nervous for, anyway? He got into the cab and pulled the brim of his old baseball cap down as he told the cab driver where he wanted to go. Max didn't say a word as they drove downtown.

It always amazed Max how bright and wondrous downtown could be. The loud traffic and the chatter of people never seemed to stop. The bright lights nearly blinded him. He had a hard time seeing these days, but downtown was always like a little Fourth of July to him.

The one thing Max could do without was the smell. In his youth, people dressed better and the city smelled a lot cleaner. These days, people were content to wallow in their filth.

*Maybe gentrification isn't such a bad thing,* Max thought as he reached his destination and got out of the cab.

Max stepped into the entryway of the strip club, paid, and nodded to the doorman as he went inside. He turned his head from side to side, scanning the dark room.

One of the girls smiled at him. "The usual, Max?"

"Yes, please."

Max took a deep breath. The young kids could have their Internet and their computers. The pictures and videos they got for free were nothing like the real thing. Sure, the computers had images and sound, but there was no taste of stale, stuffy air, or the feel of how soft and warm the women were.

Customers weren't usually allowed to touch the women, but being an old man, Max got some perks.

The young lady brought his favorite drink to him—a Jack and Coke. "Maria will see you now."

"Thank you."

Max walked across the floor and headed to one of the hallways. He was thankful when he reached it and the noise level dropped. That music they played today always gave him a headache. Maria stood outside the entrance to the private room. When she saw him, she grinned and sauntered over to him.

"Maxie!" she said, reaching up to him and kissing him on the corner of the mouth.

Max hated when people called him that. Always had, always would. Yet when Maria said it, it took him back to his youth when the air was cleaner, the prices cheaper, and the people friendlier. And to a young and beautiful woman he never forgot.

A huge grin spread across Max's face. "Maria."

She took him by the hand and led him into one of the unoccupied rooms. He sat on the chair, breathing easier now that he didn't have to put any more weight on his bum leg. He missed his cane, but he never brought it to the club. He didn't want to be reminded of the old man that he was.

They made small talk at first, about their day, but soon their words ceased. Maria began to sway her hips and dance, and she spoke a language without words—a language that aroused Max and took him to a time when he was young, strong, and full of vigor.

Maria helped Max put his wrinkly, arthritis-filled hands to her body, and he let himself be carried away to his past.

----

Mia jolted awake. She was breathing heavily, her heart pounding in her chest. She'd been dreaming of Max—the old man who lived in the apartment at the end of the hall. But she hadn't just been dreaming *about* him—in the dream, it was almost like she *was* him. She could feel how the heat rose through Max's body, and the weight of Maria on his lap, grinding against his pelvis.

*What a weird dream,* she thought. Max was a kind old man who loved to bake. Every week there were wonderful smells emanating from his apartment, and he often went door to door on the floor sharing his treats. He walked with a cane, so sometimes Mia or her boyfriend Amir helped him to carry groceries or take out his trash. Mia couldn't imagine him visiting a strip club.

As she stared up at the ceiling, Mia couldn't help but wonder why she'd dreamed of Max. Lately, Mia had been dreaming of all her neighbors—Max, Smokes A Lot Lady on the floor above her, and even that college kid who stared at her for far too long. She shivered at that last thought. He always creeped her out.

"Bad dream?" Amir mumbled from deep under the covers.

"Sorry I woke you. Not a bad dream—just a really strange one."

He stifled a yawn. "Care to share it?"

"You have to teach in the morning. You need your sleep."

"I know, but as of late, you've had a lot of fascinating dreams." He reached up and tapped her nose with his finger. She giggled. "And I can see this one's troubling you."

"They *all* trouble me."

Mia told Amir about the dream, just like she had about all the other ones. As she told it, she could once more feel the sensations Max felt. How great Maria felt against Max, and how hot it made him when she rubbed against him. It felt like more than just a dream, Mia thought, rubbing her legs against each other, her own lust rising.

"Enough talking," Mia said, rolling Amir over and climbing on top of him.

Amir had a smug smile on his face. "Are you going to show me what the dancer did?"

She stared into his dark green eyes. "Oh, I'll show you more than that."

Mia kissed Amir and the two shook off their tiredness and stayed up late into the night.

----

The next morning, Mia woke to the smell of freshly brewed coffee. She yawned before dragging herself out of bed and putting on an old, baggy shirt. She walked to their small dining room table and sat down.

Amir came over and handed her a cup of coffee. He kissed her on the forehead. "Be careful, beloved. It's hot."

"Just the way I like it. Thanks." She took a sip. "You know, I usually make coffee for you."

"I know. But you were so exhausted from last night."

She smiled. "I'm surprised you're not."

"I am, but some of us can't afford to sleep in. We don't have the luxury of working from home."

"Try not to let the little monsters devour you."

Amir grabbed his lesson plans from the table and stuffed them into his bag. He kissed her on the cheek and whispered, "I'll tell them you said that."

With her hands cupped around the warm mug, Mia watched Amir go. He might not bring in as much money as she did, but that didn't matter to her. Mia's father had left her at an early age, and all the other men she had dated or been in relationships with were very selfish and self-centered. Amir wasn't like that at all. He was far more caring and patient than anyone she had ever met. It was a wonder how he dealt with her at times, because she could be far more emotional than she ever cared to admit. He had her heart and he always would.

Mia showered and dressed, making herself look somewhat presentable before booting up the computer. Though she could wear whatever she wanted, working at home, she believed that dressing as if she were going to work put her in the proper mindset. That mind-set usually involved jeans and a T-shirt. Every once in a while, when she felt really lazy, it involved baggy sweats and a sweatshirt.

Mina spent a couple of hours on her current project before feeling the need to stretch her legs. Programming might pay the bills and allow her to work from home, but it was also boring to stare at a screen all day. She wished she had chosen a career she had passion for. Mina grabbed her coat and left their apartment. Might as well go to the store.

When Mia returned from the store, she began the long climb to their fifth-floor apartment. As usual when she was carrying anything heavy, she had to put down the bag and rest when she reached the fourth floor. She hated their place. It was entirely too small for both of them, expensive since it was in the city, and there was no elevator. She had agreed to move there because it was close to Amir's job. They both wanted to move out of the city, but he hadn't been able to find a job in the suburbs yet. Mia was anxious about it because she suspected that was when Amir would ask her to marry him. She would say yes, but Mia worried about what Amir's mother would think. His mother never did like her.

Mia picked up the bag and hauled her feet up the stairs once more. As she neared the fifth floor, she saw Ali, the little girl from the apartment next door, sitting on the stairs.

"Hey there, half-pint," Mia said, rummaging through her grocery bag. "I have a cookie for you. It's not as good as Max's—Mr. Herschel's—but I think they're the store's best."

The girl had her head down, her face hidden by her hoodie, and she didn't respond.

"Ali, what are you doing home from school so early?"

Ali looked up, her brown eyes peeking out from under her hood. "Oh, hi, Mia." She coughed. "I'm sick, so my mom said I should stay home."

Mia studied the little girl, knowing Ali had just given her a fake cough. As Mia stared at Ali, she glimpsed a dark spot on her face and she narrowed her eyes at her. "Are you all right?"

"I'm fine." The girl grinned and her voice jumped higher.

While Mia normally found that grin adorable, it was off here. There was no brightness behind Ali's smile. Children made terrible liars. Amir once said that when they tried to tell more than a little white lie, it always broke his heart. It was like watching their innocence be shattered. Mia finally realized what Amir meant.

Mia had no idea how to approach Ali. There was something going on in that household. She had always known it. She had heard the shouting coming from their apartment. There were times that Ali seemed withdrawn, and she always wore clothing that covered her body.

Mia decided to be direct. "Ali, did someone hit you?" Amir would be better at this. When she had talked to him about it before, he said they needed proof, or to witness the abuse. If they were wrong, calling social services on someone could disrupt and destroy their life. Mia was getting tired of dancing around the question. If it were true, the little girl deserved better.

Ali looked shocked. Mia couldn't tell if it was because she had been found out, or if it was because Mia had asked such a bold question.

"No!" Ali put a hand to her face. "I…ran into the door. I was being stupid and not watching where I was going, like my mother says."

Mia didn't believe her. Ali couldn't meet Mia's eyes. She was going to have to do something about this.

Mia softened her voice. "It's all right. You can tell me if anything's wrong."

The girl clenched her fists and bit the inside of her lip. Her eyes finally met Mia's and she opened her mouth.

"Ali!" a voice shouted through the hallway. "You get in here, right now!"

"Coming, Dad!" She leaped up, and Mia grabbed her hand.

"Remember what I said."

Ali nodded.

"And here's a cookie."

"Thanks," Ali said. She gave Mia that sincere, full-of-life smile that warmed Mia's heart, before running back home.

Mia glared in the direction Ali had gone. When she reached the top of the stairs, she caught a glimpse of Ali's father standing by the doorway. Their eyes met and she gave him an icy stare. He returned it before shutting the door.

As Mia put away the groceries, she couldn't help but think of Ali and her father, Bill. Work didn't ease Mia's mind, and she was still tired from last night's activities. Mia crashed on the loveseat and took a nap.

# CHAPTER 2

MIA DREAMED of Ali. She towered over the little girl and watched as Ali sat at the kitchen table with a mouth full of cereal. It took Mia a second to notice that Ali was wearing the same red hoodie. With a shock, she realized that she wasn't dreaming. That what she was witnessing was real.

With Ali's hood down, the bruise on her face was clearly visible. That bruise angered Mia. *Why would someone do this to her?* Mia thought.

"Finish your food, then clean up the dishes," Mia found herself saying. Yet, it wasn't Mia who spoke. It was Ali's mother, Kate.

Kate was always a bit too uptight for Mia. Her blond hair was never out of place and her business suits never seemed to have a wrinkle. Mia didn't think she was human. But that wasn't what bothered Mia. Mia didn't think Kate was warm and caring like a mother should be. Not that Mia's own mother was like that. If there was one word Mia would use to describe Kate, it would be "cold."

Ali got out of her seat and carried the bowl toward the sink. She slipped on the way there. She managed to hold onto the bowl, but the little bit of milk that was left splashed out.

"What did you do?" Kate's voice had gotten low and menacing.

Ali flinched. "I'm—I'm sorry, Mom. I didn't mean to."

"You never mean to. I have an important lunch meeting to go to and you almost spilled milk on my suit. You're so clumsy!" Kate stalked toward her daughter.

Bill came into the dining room and spoke in a soft voice. "Kate, please. She meant nothing by it. Look, she's going to clean it up right now."

Kate gave Bill a look that silenced him. "And you should be out there finding a job. The only thing worse than marrying an idiot is marrying a lazy bum." Bill cast his eyes down and slowly backed away.

Mia was surprised at how much anger lurked inside of Kate. She felt Kate's anger not only at her daughter and husband, but at Kate herself. The coldness Mia always felt radiating from Kate was made to hold back the storm. Right now, the storm was building inside of Kate, and Mia was along for the ride. Kate tried not to let her emotions overwhelm her, but the one good thing in her life—her family—didn't help matters.

Ali hurried and grabbed a couple of paper towels. She wiped the milk from the floor, but the towels weren't absorbent enough. They tore and fell apart.

Kate knocked Ali to the side and the little girl tumbled to the floor. "You're useless! Always have been. Why do I have to put up with you?" Kate raised her hand to strike her daughter, and Ali shut her eyes and cringed.

That rage that Kate felt had finally boiled over. It also affected Mia, but she didn't feel it towards Ali or even Bill. She felt it at Kate, for wanting to strike at her lovely daughter, and how Kate didn't seem to understand how lucky she was. Some people would have killed for a daughter like that.

"No!" Mia shouted with her mind.

Kate's arm paused in midflight. Mia stared at Kate's hand. Her hand. Slowly, she moved it back and forth. She was completely in control of Kate's body.

----

The alarm on Mia's phone shocked her and tore her from Kate's body. She turned the alarm off and leaned forward, her elbows on her knees.

Somehow, while she was asleep on her couch, her consciousness had transferred into Kate's body. And last night—had she really been in Max's body? How could this be possible? What did it mean? Could she do it when she was awake? If so, what could she do with this ability?

For the rest of the day, Mia could think of nothing else but her newfound abilities. As she straightened up the apartment and took out the trash, her mind was filled with questions.

When Mia reached the trash chute, she saw Ali there. "Hey, half-pint."

Ali was startled and dropped her trash. The bag spilled open and garbage scattered everywhere.

"I'm sorry," Ali said, flinching. "It was an accident."

"Don't be sorry," Mia said as she bent down to help Ali. "It was my fault. I shouldn't have startled you."

Mia swept up the damp paper towels, eggshells, and open packages, not caring that her hands became soiled. It was her fault, after all, and Ali didn't deserve what had happened to her. She tried not to stare at Ali's bruise, but she couldn't help it. The girl didn't notice that her hood was down and that Mia could clearly see what had happened to her.

The more Mia stared at Ali's bruise, the more her anger rose. Anger at what Kate did to Ali, and at how Bill did nothing to stop it. She had been wrong about Bill. He wasn't the one who caused the abuse, but he was just as guilty.

Ali caught her staring and turned her head away, fumbling with her hoodie.

Mia grabbed her arm. "It's all right. It's not your fault. Things will get better for you. I promise." Mia had no idea how, but she knew she could make it happen with her newfound power.

It nearly broke Mia's heart when Ali gave her that hopeful look that children gave freely. Ali's parents hadn't broken that spirit yet. But the small smile Ali showed wasn't as bright as it once was.

"Go, now," Mia said. "Your parents are waiting."

Ali turned to leave, but stopped. She ran back to Mia and hugged her so hard that Mia felt the ache in her body. Mia tried not to get her garbage-covered hands on Ali when she returned the hug. But the girl squeezed so tightly and with so much love that Mia stopped caring about getting Ali's clothes dirty, and Mia soon found herself returning the hug with as much ferocity as Ali.

"I wish you were my mother," Ali whispered. The little girl pulled away from her and ran back home.

A tear slid from Mia's eye. She shook her head to clear it and wished that what Ali said was true. Then a smile crept onto Mia's face. Maybe Ali's wish could come true...in a way.

Mia slacked off work for the rest of the day. She'd catch up tomorrow—at least that's what she told herself. What she tried to do was slip into Kate's body again. But she wasn't able to. She shut off all distractions in her place—the TV, the radio, the computer. She even took the batteries out of the wall clock and unplugged the refrigerator for complete silence. She tried to slow her breathing to focus her mind, like she had seen in movies, but nothing worked. Frustrated, Mia decided to blow off some steam and go to the gym. When Amir returned home from work, she'd talk to him about it. She just hoped she didn't seem too crazy to him. But if she couldn't trust the man she loved more than anything with this, then what could she trust him with?

Because Mia made good money and because she was a terrible cook, the couple ordered takeout and ate out a lot. They were also near a lot of good food places—one of the advantages of living in the city. Amir was an excellent cook, but he was often exhausted when he got home and didn't feel like cooking. He only cooked once or twice a week.

Mia had dinner ready when he got home. It was Thai from their favorite spot about two blocks away. During dinner, Mia told Amir all about what happened to Ali, and what happened to Mia. Amir stopped eating his pai thai and stared at Mia. His dark green eyes bored into her, making her shiver. That thoughtful, smoldering look made him very sexy, but she pushed that thought aside. She just hoped that he would believe her. It sounded so crazy.

Amir was sitting as still as a statue with a vacant look on his face, his eyes not blinking.

"Amir?" Mia asked, worried that he didn't seem to be breathing. She placed a hand on his, and he moved suddenly. He startled her and she jumped.

"Sorry," he said, his eyes coming to focus on her. "I was just mulling over what you said. It's…"

"Crazy," she said, her eyes downcast.

He sighed and patted her hand. "A lot to take in. Having your soul leave your body and take over others? I've seen and read about some amazing things in the world, but nothing like that. But it would explain the dreams you've had recently, if it were true." He paused, deep in thought again. Finally he said, "If you could do it when you were awake, then we could be sure it was really happening. Are you sure you can't?"

Mia shook her head. "I told you. I tried earlier today."

Amir scratched his cheek, a thoughtful expression on his face. "There has to be a way to test if what you say is true. You might just be having really vivid dreams."

"No," she said, her jaw tightening. "They're more than that. I tell you, they're *real*."

"I believe that you believe what you say, but you have to admit, it sounds a little unbelievable." He added quickly, "I still love you."

Mia yanked her hand away and clenched her fist. How she wanted to wipe that kind smile from Amir's face. Before she could say something she might regret, there was a knock at the door.

Even though Mia was closer to the door, Amir knew it was best if he got away from the table and answered it.

"Good evening, Mr. Herschel," Amir said. His eyes wandered to the basket in Max's hand. "What brings you by?"

"I made these chocolate chip cookies," Max said, holding up the basket. "And thought they would be great for your dessert." He made a sad face when he saw the store-bought cookies on the counter. "Oh. I guess you don't need these."

"No, wait," Amir said, grabbing Max's arm. "Those cookies Mia bought are trash compared to yours."

"I heard that!" Mia said.

Max smiled and handed over four cookies. "Two for each of you."

"Thank you, sir."

Max turned to leave, but Amir stopped him. "Mr. Herschel, I have a small favor to ask you. My friend is getting married and before he does, he would like one last wild night on the town. I was wondering if you knew of any…establishments that we could frequent?"

Max glanced past Amir to Mia, and then lowered his voice and leaned in like he and Amir were sharing a secret. "You mean, hoochie clubs?"

"That's right," Amir said, suppressing a smile at the term "hoochie." "Like in the movies? I've spent a few years in America but I've not had many opportunities to go to one. I thought you might know, since you've lived your whole life in this city."

"Well, now, that's not at all the kind of place I would go to myself," Max said with a sly grin. "You understand."

Amir nodded. "Of course not," he agreed solemnly.

"But I have a few buddies who talk about this place called the Hot Box. You might try there." Max gave Amir a wink. "If you want your friend to have a real good time, ask for Maria." The old man turned away and began to make his way down the hall, leaning on his cane.

"Thanks for the cookies," Amir called, watching him go.

Mia sidled up to Amir and snatched a cookie from his hand. She had a wry smile on her face. "The Hot Box. That's the place I saw in my dream. And I told you the girl's name was Maria. Do you believe me now?"

Amir glanced at her before peering down the hall one last time. He'd truly been shocked when Max's recommendation matched what Mia had told him. "I guess I do. I just don't understand how you can do it."

She shrugged. "Me neither, but it seems I can."

"We don't know the extent of your abilities." Amir's eyebrows furrowed. "This could be dangerous for you. I'm worried." Amir walked away from the door and went to his phone. "The good thing about this is now we *know* what's happening to Ali—we don't have to worry about raising false suspicions. We need to call Social Services and have them open an investigation as soon as possible. Obviously we can't tell them that you witnessed the abuse, but we can tell them about the bruises—and say that we're pretty sure it's Kate that's doing it. Thank Allah we didn't report Bill. Not that he's a good parent for letting this happen, but we could have ruined things for him and Ali."

"Hold on," Mia said. "Can we wait on it?"

Amir studied Mia for a minute, and then he sighed. "What do you plan to do?"

"I've been thinking about this. I want to see if I can change Kate...or at least make things better for Ali."

"You don't even know if you can control Kate's body again."

"You might be right, but I have to try."

Amir said carefully, "Beloved, even assuming you can control Kate's body again, I believe this is wrong. You can't just take control of another person and take away their free will. We need to get Ali out of there, not try to change her mother."

"You don't know what it's like growing up without a mother!" Mia shouted. Tears hovered on the edges of her eyes.

That froze Amir. Mia's mother had killed herself when Mia was just a child, but it was a subject Mia never talked about.

"Please, Amir. Ali deserves a caring mother. If I can get Kate to change, then maybe I can give Ali the childhood I never had."

"All right," he said. He opened up his arms and Mia fell into them. "We'll try it your way. But I want you to know that I'm against this. You can't be inside Kate all the time, and you don't know what being inside her will do to her—or you."

"I have to try."

"I know how headstrong you are—you'll do this no matter what I say. But if this makes things worse, we're finding another way of getting Ali out of there. As a teacher, I can't let Ali be abused anymore."

"Agreed. Neither of us wants that."

Amir hugged her tighter and whispered into her ear, "You may be going about this wrong. Maybe you were able to do...whatever it is you do because you were relaxed. Maybe you need to put yourself at ease and not force your way in."

---

*Amir was right,* Mia thought, letting herself drift away on the edge of sleep. She didn't need to force it. It wasn't like she was stealing their bodies; it was more like she was slipping into their bodies. *Like a new set of clothes. Old set,* she corrected herself.

And like putting on a set of clothes, Mia felt Kate's body adjust to her. Kate was sitting in front of a laptop with a bunch of work emails open. Mia wiggled Kate's fingers before closing the laptop.

Now that Mia was the driver instead of a passenger, she had expected something different. Maybe movies and TV shows were to blame, but she feared she might hear Kate's voice in the back of her head, begging for Mia to get out of her body. But there was only silence.

Mia eyed Bill as he sat in his recliner, watching TV. When she got up, she could see

Bill glance at her from the corner of his eye, but he made no move to stop her. She moved toward Ali's room, knowing that she would find Ali asleep but still wanting to see her. Mia found walking oddly difficult. Kate was taller than Mia, and Mia wasn't used to her long strides. Kate was also slimmer and more athletic, as opposed to Mia's curvier figure. Mia unbuttoned the top two buttons of Kate's pajamas, which she found stifling. *Jesus, does that woman always have to be so stiff?*

When Mia opened the door, instead of a slumbering Ali, she found Ali under the covers with a light. Mia smiled when she saw the little girl reading. Ali scrambled and turned out the light, and then stilled her body.

"Ali, what are you doing?"

Ali peeked out from under her covers and said, "I—I couldn't sleep."

Mia was shocked by the look of fear on Ali's face, but then she remembered whose body she inhabited. She softened her voice and treated Ali like a frightened animal who she was scared to run off. She sat down on the bed next to her, getting close but not too close.

"What are you reading?" Mia asked.

"Ummm…"

"Which one?" Mia asked, her voice hardening and coming out like Kate's.

Ali's hand shook as she took the hidden book from under her covers and handed it to her mother. The book was a very used and tattered copy of *Matilda*.

Mia smiled as she ran her fingers over the lettering. She remembered giving this book to Ali. It was one of her favorite childhood books. She was glad that Ali had been reading it. Still, if she had known what Ali's parents were like she might not have given Ali the book, considering the subject matter.

Mia handed the book back to Ali. "Are you enjoying it?"

Ali nodded.

"Would you like me to read you some?"

The little girl's mouth hung open and her eyes were wide. "Yes," she squeaked.

Mia smiled as she opened the book and began to read her favorite story to her favorite little girl.

----

When Mia opened her own eyes and finally slipped out of Kate's body, she felt like jumping out of her bed and screaming in excitement, but she didn't want to wake Amir. She could spend time with Ali and make sure that Kate treated her right. She could also slip into Bill's body and keep an eye on Kate.

Mia continued to watch over Ali and be her mother, but only when her own body slept. She still hadn't figured out how to do it when she was awake. As much as she loved being Ali's mother, another part of her loved that she got to practice and hone her abilities.

Thursday nights, Ali would come over to eat dinner, watch TV, or play board games. Kate usually worked late Thursday nights, and that was the day that Amir also cooked.

The next Thursday there was a knock at the door, and Mia went to answer.

"Hey, half-pint," Mia said. "You're early."

Ali looked up at Mia with a sad expression on her face. "I'm sorry."

Mia bent down to her. "For what?"

The little girl pulled her hands from behind her back. In them were the tattered remains of *Matilda*.

Mia gasped. "Oh, no. What happened?"

Ali's words were barely audible. "My mom. She's been reading it to me and when she came home early to take a shower, I asked her to read it to me again." Ali's voice grew louder and she talked faster. "She said she hasn't been reading to me and when I said she has every night, she got mad. That's when she took my book from me and tore it into pieces. I'm sorry."

"Oh, it's not your fault, half-pint. It's your mother's. She shouldn't have destroyed your property. I'll get you another copy." She tried not to show Ali how upset she was. She hadn't thought about what might happen as a result of her mingling with Kate. It was as if Ali had to deal with Dr. Jekyll and Mr. Hyde for a mother. Mia whispered, "Hey, you might want to be careful around your mother for a while. Try not to make her mad or do anything that will upset her unless she comes to you and is nice. She may act...differently at times."

"It's her meds. That's what my dad says."

Mia paused. That would explain a lot. She ruffled Ali's hair. "Can you do that for me?"

Ali nodded.

"And I'll get you another book as soon as I—"

"Ali! What are you doing?" Kate stormed down the hallway to Mia's apartment. She pulled Ali backwards and Mia rose to face her neighbor. "I want you to leave my child alone," Kate said. "You and your terrorist boyfriend are a bad influence. Giving my child a book about a girl with telekinetic powers. What kind of drivel are you filling my child's head with?"

Amir came out from the kitchen, using a dish towel to dry his hands. "What's with all the shouting? Dinner's almost ready."

Mia glanced at Amir and silenced him. Then she focused her fierce gaze on Kate. Instead of letting herself slide into Kate's body, the anger fueled Mia and she pushed herself forcefully inside of Kate. Mia's mind screamed out from pain and her body collapsed.

"Mia!" Ali yelled, and pushed past her mother to Mia.

Amir rushed to catch Mia. "Ali, get my phone and call 9-1-1. We've got to—"

"She's fine," Kate said.

"No, Mom. We have to help her."

"Ali, put the phone down," Amir said, understanding passing between him and Mia. "Please. I'll see that she gets help. I promise."

The little girl hesitated before putting the phone down.

Mia, in Kate's body, bent down to Ali and softly grabbed her shoulders. In a gentle voice, she said, "It's going to be all right, half—Ali. I'm sorry for what I did. Let's go home. Once I'm gone, you can come over to Mia's and Amir's for dinner and to check in on her. I'm sure she'd like that."

Ali followed her mother, then stopped and looked back at Mia with a worried expression on her face.

"It's all right," Amir said. "She'll be fine."

Ali nodded before taking off back toward her apartment.

Amir sighed and laid his girlfriend on the couch. He placed a pillow under her head and asked softly, "Beloved, what did you do?"

Mia, in Kate's body, put her fingers to her temples. Her skull was throbbing. She knew it came from her taking over Kate's body in such a fashion, but Mia had to do it. Kate had ripped up her own daughter's book and insulted Amir. The anger in Mia had boiled over until she took over Kate's body.

Mia was going to have to be more careful with Ali and Kate now. She was also going to have to practice slipping into bodies while she was awake, but at least now she knew she could use her ability while awake. She needed to get back to Amir. He could be such a worrywart at times. But first she had to watch Kate. She decided to try something different. Instead of going into her own body first, she decided to leap into Bill's body from Kate's.

When Mia slipped out of Kate's body and into Bill—the Couch Potato, as she'd started thinking of him—it didn't hurt as much as taking over Kate's body. There was some resistance, but it felt more like putting on a new shoe. It was stiff and hurt a little, but the more she stayed inside, the more she got used to it.

Kate glanced around her apartment with a baffled expression on her face. "What am I doing here?"

Mia studied Kate. As often as she'd taken over bodies, she'd never witnessed what happened after she left one. It was just as Mia suspected. They never even knew Mia had been there. There was a gap in their memory and they experienced disorientation and confusion.

A smile crept onto Mia's face. *Perfect.*

Mia awoke in her own body, to the smell of falafel. "Thank God. I'm starving," she said, rising from the couch.

Amir stopped cooking, wiped his hands, and walked over to her. He hugged her tightly and said, "I was so worried about you. I thought something happened to you, but then I realized you slid into Kate." He put his hands to her face. "You've got to be more careful, beloved."

She fell into his embrace. "I know. But she just made me so mad. First at what she did to the book I gave Ali, and then by calling you a terrorist. That bitch deserves more."

"Maybe so, but we'll have to do it legally. Can you keep an eye on her?"

She nodded. "I can do that and much more." Mia told Amir that she didn't have to be in her own body to go into another's.

"I wonder what else I can do?" Mia asked.

"I think you should be more careful."

"I won't get into any trouble, now that I know what I'm doing."

"No," Amir said, grabbing her shoulders. "I mean for your soul. I'm worried. Does this mean you're now unanchored and aren't tied to a body? I know you aren't religious, but I can't help but be concerned."

Mia put a gentle hand to his face. "You're sweet, but I'll be fine."

There was a knock at the door.

"I'll get the door," she said. "It's probably Ali. Is dinner ready?"

Amir's eyes widened. "Shoot! I was so worried about you, things might have gotten a little overcooked."

He dashed back to the kitchen, and Mia smiled and shook her head. Soul. She didn't believe in any of that, but she was definitely going to have to see just what the extent of her abilities were.

# CHAPTER 3

*God, this is so boring,* Mia thought, blowing a strand of hair out of her face. She sat at her computer, working, but she couldn't concentrate. She wanted to get out into the city and be free.

Over the last week, Mia had been practicing her ability. She'd learned that she was only able to go into someone's body if they were less than thirty feet away, forty if she pushed it. But doing that brought a terrible headache and blood trickled out of her nose. Thirty feet was far enough, she'd decided. What use did she have for slipping into someone's body from so far away anyway?

She also learned something that hadn't disturbed her as much as she thought it should have. Whenever she left her body, it was like she was a puppet and someone cut her strings—her body collapsed. When she practiced it at her apartment, she soon realized she had to be careful. She didn't want her body to suffer an injury, or worse.

It wasn't long before she started practicing her abilities outside of their home. She wanted to move beyond those bodies in her apartment building, especially since she was getting to know her neighbors a bit too well. Amir once told her that he loved to people-watch, especially when he came to America. To him, America was just a great melting pot. People with all sorts of differences and backgrounds came to America to build a better future for their families.

Mia didn't see what he saw, but still his idealistic view gave her an idea. She'd practice her ability while sitting on a park bench or by the fountain in front of the government building downtown. No one seemed to notice or care about a young woman slumped over in those places—they probably assumed she'd just fallen asleep.

Mia needed a break from work and thought about going outside to hone her abilities again. Her ability was freeing in a way, but she felt she could do more with her powers. She decided to watch TV instead, hoping the court shows would amuse her. She always loved the fake courtroom drama. But instead of being relieved by the mindless arguing of humanity, she found that the channel was another boring news report.

Amir must have left the TV tuned to one of his news channels. She'd never understood his fascination with watching the news. Maybe it was because he was from another country, and the workings of the US government were still interesting to him. She was tired of all the lies those in charge of the country told.

Mia reached for the remote, getting ready to change the channel, when the news reporter spoke of yet another scandal involving the CEO of a major company. If Mia were honest with herself, she didn't quite understand all the fancy terms the reporter used, but she did know one thing—this man had stolen hard-earned money from the people his company was supposed to help and serve. If it weren't for those people, the man wouldn't have received millions of dollars in the first place.

"James Calvin," she whispered to herself, staring at the image of the man on the screen. An idea began to form in her head.

Mia flung the remote back on the couch, letting the news channel stay on, and she quickly went back to her computer. She searched for all the information she could find on James Calvin. He was in his early 40s, lived in the city with his wife, and had three grown children. When she dug a little deeper, she found that James Calvin had funneled millions of dollars from the people's accounts, disguising them as so-called maintenance fees, convenience fees, handling charges, service charges and the like. People didn't question those charges and fees because over the years they had gotten used to paying them, when it was in fact *their* own money that made the banks and corporations their millions and billions. There were also rumors that Calvin had affairs, not that that surprised her. The most frustrating thing was that because of his expensive lawyers, it looked like he was going to get off easy.

Mia forced herself to stop reading about him, as the more she read, the more it angered her. There always seemed to be a company stealing millions, police brutalizing people, politicians lying, and people being forced out of their homes. It maddened her. She smiled as she thought about Amir. The same things impassioned him too, but unlike her, he believed he could still make a difference with voting and supporting the right people. Mia had given up on the system and believing she could change it long ago.

Amir returned home. He hung up his coat and took off his shoes. "Sorry I'm late. The bus ran into a bit of traffic."

A wisp of a smile crossed Mia's face. The bus he rode to work was where they'd first met. They still rode it together from time to time, for no reason except to be with each other. They rode together much less often now, since she worked at home, but it was their thing, and it would always be their thing.

"There was a crowd of people protesting," Amir said. "It made traffic hell." He went to her and kissed her on the cheek. "But I'm home now."

She returned the kiss and smiled. "What were they protesting?"

"I don't know if you've watched the news—probably not—but there is another financial fraud trial. James Calvin stole millions through his bank, charging people with made-up fees to use their money." Amir shook his head and sighed. "It's hard to tell what fees are real and what are made up anymore. I hope to learn more, as I'll be watching it in the weeks to come."

She smirked. "I'll never understand how this fascinates you so much."

He smiled back at her. "You have your courtroom dramas, I have mine." He pulled out his phone. "Pizza tonight? The usual?"

"Sounds good to me." Mia moved to the couch and said, "Hey, I have a question for you. What do you think will happen to Calvin?"

He paused in the middle of dialing his phone. "I'd like to think that the judicial system will consider all the options, and he'll get what he deserves. However, you've taught me that will not be the case."

"Yet you don't seem worried about him getting away scot-free."

"That's because I have faith, beloved. Whether or not James Calvin gets off from the American justice system, it doesn't matter. He'll get what's coming to him."

Normally, Mia would roll her eyes at Amir's misplaced optimism. As endearing as she found it, one could only take so much, especially when it came to listening to him drone on and on about karma. Mia wasn't sure if she believed in karma, but she did believe that men like James Calvin shouldn't get off without some kind of punishment.

*Bad people shouldn't be able to get away with whatever they want,* Mia thought. *Maybe karma just needs a little push.*

----

Amir was right. The trial of James Calvin had devolved into a media circus. Mia was tempted to just ride into other people's bodies to get to the courthouse. It was far easier than walking and taking the bus, but she had neglected her body too much. She felt like she might have gained five pounds, and it had been at least a week since she last went to the gym.

Mia waited with the rest of the people. She ignored the protestors and news reporters, wrapping her arms around herself. The city's wind always had a bite to it this time of year, but the changing colors of the leaves almost made it worth it. Almost. She wished Amir was there, wrapping his strong arms around her, but she knew he would try to stop her if he found out what she planned.

"Finally," she said to herself, after waiting for hours. She should have taken someone else's body. Maybe a fatter one that could have withstood the cold better, or an athletic one that could have stood up for days. But no, Mia wanted to stare into James Calvin's eyes with her own. She believed that she could get a better understanding of the man if she did, and if she didn't like what she saw, then and only then would she use her ability.

Mia pushed forward through the crowd as much as she could. Between the police, media security, barricades, and protesting people, she didn't get too far. She was able to hear bits and pieces of what Calvin said to the media. Those words were a rehash of all the same lies she had heard before. What he'd done was a mistake. He made wrong investments and things got out of hand. Blah, blah, blah. The words became like the crowd, just background noise to her.

"Come on," Mia said, wanting to see his dark blue eyes.

As Calvin spoke to the press and the people, his words were clear and he didn't stutter or trip over what he said. He spoke to the crowd and when he turned his head, his eyes met Mia's. The older man briefly smiled at her before moving on. In another life, Mia might have found him attractive. As their eyes met, to her, their gaze lasted far longer than a second. He was too far away for her to slip into his body, but she knew his intentions.

"Liar," she said, her own eyes hardening. She had no doubt that Calvin was a snake in the grass. That he knew exactly what he was doing when he committed those crimes. She knew that he would get off and commit the same crimes again. Mia had always been good at reading people, but now that she could literally get inside someone, she believed she was better at it. Maybe that's why she had those abilities.

Whether it was fate, God, or a freak accident, it didn't matter to Mia. She was going to use her gifts to help people, or, if they did something wrong, to stop them.

----

Over the next few days, Mia let her work suffer as she followed James Calvin. She didn't take her own body because she didn't want to be seen. She trailed Calvin, leaping from body to body, leaving confused people in her wake. It was hard for her because she had to work around Amir's schedule. One night he had to work late, and that was when Mia was finally able to follow Calvin home. She had come up with a plan, but she was going to need more than a few hours to make it work.

To enact her plan, Mia had to do the one thing she hated to do—lie to Amir. She told him she was going to a programmers conference. She did go to them a few times a year, and they were the most boring things she'd ever been to.

Mia booked a motel room well away from the places Amir frequented, and nowhere near Calvin. Mia settled into her room, then peeked through the window blinds. Night had fallen and she was thankful for it. The part of the city she was in wasn't the friendliest area, but the night had a way of masking how dirty and grimy it was. The crisp, cool air carried away the smell of stale urine and unwashed people. With what Mia could do, she was no longer afraid of this part of the city. She was the predator instead of the prey.

Mia reached for the last of her Vietnamese noodles and slurped them. As bad, dirty, and smelly as this part of the city could be, they had some of the most delicious food here. Go figure.

"Time to get to work," she said.

Mia moved to the lumpy motel bed and lay down. She closed her eyes and unanchored her body, moving to the one next door. Like a subway or bus system, Mia used the bodies to travel, barely staying more than a split second before moving on to the next one. She was soon outside, hitching on those riding in the cars along the street. Because of the light traffic, how far away she was, and how she had to calculate and figure out where people were going, it took her two hours to move five miles through the city. When the person she was in was on the street to Calvin's house, that's when Mia took over.

The midsized car swerved as Mia took control. She quickly corrected herself, just before she smashed into an oncoming car.

"Whew," Mia said, wiping her sweaty forehead. She might have gotten adept at forcing her way into bodies, but controlling them was still jarring. The seatbelt pushed against her large frame, and her right hand ached. *Arthritis,* Mia thought.

Mia pulled the car over, double parking in a red zone. She stared at the door to Calvin's home and waited. She had been tracking Calvin's movements and knew he always came home late. She wanted to take control of his body, and this was when he'd be the most vulnerable.

It wasn't the best plan of action, but she didn't want to take over the maid or butler's life, Calvin's lawyer or driver, or even some random stranger. Dealing with Ali's mother had taught Mia that her actions could have grave repercussions. Sure, she could easily slip away, but they couldn't. They'd have to deal with what she'd done, and she needed to control them for this to work, not just be a passenger. No, this plan, as shaky as is was, only allowed one person to get hurt, the one she was after—James Calvin.

The fat fingers on her steering wheel drummed. Mia had grown tired of waiting. She'd thought Calvin would be home in at most an hour. Instead, three hours passed— and nothing. Mia had to ignore the texts and phone calls the woman she occupied had received. Finally, a car pulled up in front of Calvin's house, and she knew it to be Calvin's.

Mia closed her eyes and strained to use her ability. The pressure in her head intensified until she finally left the body she'd borrowed and slipped into Calvin's. Mia grabbed the car door to steady herself. It always took her a few seconds longer to adjust to a man's body. Men were just so big, awkward, and hairy.

"Are you all right, sir?" the driver asked.

"Yes," Mia said, fiddling with her crimson tie. She cleared her throat. "I'm fine. Thank you. That will be all."

Mia walked to the front door. She barely restrained herself from bouncing. Whatever she might think of James Calvin, he took good care of himself. Men might lack the agile, flexible, sensual feeling of a woman, but they did have strength.

At the door, Mia paused with the keys in her hand. There were nearly a dozen of them, and she fumbled for the correct one. Her heart began to beat faster when she couldn't find the right one. Maybe this was a bad idea. Maybe she shouldn't have—

The door opened and an elderly man with a British accent said, "May I help you, sir?"

From his uniform, Mia could see that this was the butler. She had studied James Calvin and the immediate family around him, but you could only learn so much from reading and watching interviews. Even though Mia could have hidden in their bodies or James's, she never had. There was always that nagging fear that they would catch her, even though that was impossible. Plus, there was a feeling that she might see something that could change her mind about going through with her grand plan.

Mia tried to remember the butler's name, but couldn't. She began to panic and needed to take deep breaths.

"Are you all right, sir?" he asked, moving closer to her.

"I'm…fine." *I can do this,* she thought. *I have to, before he gets off and the world forgets about his crimes.* Her breathing slowed and she said, "Thank you, Stephen."

She shuffled past the butler, shielding her eyes from the blinding light. The light seemed to bounce from everywhere. The walls, tables, and the other furniture were pristine and devoid of any personality. Gold leaf covered and decorated the edges of practically everything. Did Calvin think he was King Midas?

"Tacky."

"Sir?"

"That'll be all," Mia said. She straightened herself and stood taller. She had to remember who she was. She was no longer Mia, a computer programmer. She was James Calvin, a man who made millions, who prided himself on his appearance, and who stole money from people.

"Good night, sir."

"Good night, Stephen."

Mia walked up the stairs, trying not to gawk at everything. The vases, the candleholders, the carpet—everything was worth a mint. She paused when she got to the top, her hand leaning on the banister. As Mia turned her head and stared down the hallway, she thought the inside of the house looked a lot bigger than the outside.

However, a man like Calvin would keep the information Mia needed in an office, bedroom, or phone. She took the phone out, but when she tried to use it the screen was locked. She thought about letting Calvin take control, but he would be disoriented and wonder why he was here. No, she would have to do this alone. If she couldn't succeed, she'd merely come back another time.

Mia paused, realizing that she had become far more comfortable with being in Calvin's body for an extended period of time and going through with her plan. *I can get used to this.*

Mia appeared to be alone…aside from the butler, and she remembered reading about a maid, and possibly even a cook. *How lazy are rich people?* Despite being relatively alone, Mia hurried through the house, searching for the information she needed. She finally found the office at the end of the long hallway.

She booted up the computer and as she waited for it to start, she rummaged through the drawers of the desk. Mia found plenty of bills, but those weren't the financials she was looking for. The computer finally started and as her eyes went to the screen, she said, "Damn."

The computer, like the phone, was password protected. Mia slammed her hands down on the desk. This was getting frustrating. She was going to have to come back another day. If only she were a hacker, not a programmer, maybe she'd have better luck. Calvin was older than Mia but still relatively young. Surely he didn't keep all of his secrets and information on a computer. With the news focused on him lately, the Robin Hood hacker groups might think James Calvin a tempting target.

Mia started to peek behind all the beautiful paintings in his office. It was as good an idea as any she'd have. However, none of the paintings had a safe behind them. She remembered all the ones she'd passed on the way here, not to mention ones that could be in the other rooms. There were a lot more paintings she'd have to look behind. And even if she did find a safe, how would she open it? She exhaled in frustration, thinking that a lock of hair would blow away from her face as it had so many times before. But there was nothing there. Men didn't have long hair. Well, most men anyway.

"What *are* you doing?"

Mia froze, hearing the woman's voice behind her. She turned, trying to remember that she belonged there, since she was in James Calvin's body.

An attractive woman with an exquisite, blinding necklace stood in the doorway. Her dark blue gown shimmered as she moved her blond hair to take off her earrings. Her body was firm and slim, except in the right spots. Her skin and figure looked too good for her not to have had any work done, but Mia couldn't tell. Mia remembered that this was Calvin's wife.

"James, are you going to answer me?"

Mia wished she could remember the woman's name. Instead, she focused on trying to figure out whether or not to lie to her. The woman's shrewd blue eyes told Mia that that would be a bad idea. Women were always one step ahead of men.

"I'm sorry," Mia said, thinking of Amir. "I was taken aback by your beauty."

"Please." The woman rolled her eyes, yet Mia caught the hint of a smile. "Isabella is going to have to clean up your mess in the morning. What are you looking for?"

"Forgive me, Natasha," Mia said, finally remembering her name. "I…can't seem to remember my password." She decided to tell the shrewd wife the truth. There was also a chance that, much like Amir, Calvin might let Natasha be in charge of the finances...legal finances at any rate. *We're far better at numbers than men,* Mia thought.

Natasha sighed and shook her head. "Your piece of antiquated password paper is in the place it's always in."

Mia glanced around the room. She had no idea where that would be. "Which is?"

"I swear," Natasha said, rolling her eyes. "If your board and stockholders knew how much of a Luddite you were, you'd have been fired long ago. Good thing you're skilled at reading people. If you hadn't stolen their money, the people would be laughing at you."

Mia gasped. She felt a moment of triumph. She was right. James Calvin *had* been deliberately stealing money from people. There would be no more hesitation in Mia from now on, as she enacted the rest of her plan.

Mia stared at Natasha as she watched James's wife walk to the desk and fish out a piece of paper that was taped under the drawer. She walked back over to Mia and stuck the piece of paper out. "Here. It's where you always leave it."

As Mia looked at the paper, she had a hard time making out the chicken scratch. There were nearly a dozen passwords and names of sites from banks, financial organizations, email, and credit cards.

"Thank you," Mia said. "What would I do without you?" She leaned forward to give Natasha a kiss.

Natasha pulled back and said, "James, what are you doing?"

"I was going to thank you." Mia smiled. Natasha was a strikingly beautiful woman and she was curious about kissing her.

"Have you been drinking again?" Natasha pulled away farther. "Now is not the time, with the trial. We're alone and don't have to keep up appearances." She walked away. "Go have fun with one of your little tramps, and I will have my own fun. Whatever you do, keep it discreet, especially now."

As Mia watched her go, she realized that all of the rumors about James's affairs were true. However, despite all that, Mia was more interested in Natasha. She'd thought that Natasha was just another pretty wife who stood by her husband throughout all the trials and tribulations. She was more. Mia's plan might also destroy Natasha, but Natasha had done nothing to stop James. She was just as guilty.

Mia shook her head before heading to the desk. Natasha was a strong woman. She would survive.

Though things were not progressing as Mia would have liked, her plan was a simple one. Much like her favorite childhood story, ·*Robin Hood* (the one with Costner) she would rob from the rich and give to the poor. Her plan was to distribute as much of the wealth as she could, and make it so Calvin couldn't merely get it back. She would also write a very heartfelt and touching apology and send it to various media outlets. A part of Mia hoped that because of it, James Calvin would turn over a new leaf, but she highly doubted it.

The plan took Mia late into the night. Transferring and dispersing money, even digitally, took forever. And with James Calvin there was a lot of it. She knew she couldn't get rid of all of it, but she hoped that she had gotten rid of enough. Then she had to change all the passwords afterward to make sure that James couldn't easily reverse the transactions. Lastly, Mia couldn't help but make a charitable donation to herself. A finder's fee for all the good, hard work she'd had to do.

As tired as Mia was and as late as it got, she still had one final thing to do. That blasted letter. She stared at the bright screen, trying to figure out what to say.

"Oh God," Mia said. "I'm not a writer." She yawned, glancing at the clock overhead. It wasn't her body, but she still felt exhausted. James Calvin needed to rest. But her work wasn't done.

Mia began to type what she had originally planned. A paragraph in, she decided that what she was writing was too cold. This was supposed to be James Calvin's swan song—a final atonement. It had to be more heartfelt. Mia didn't know if Calvin actually cared about what he'd done to those people, but he had to sound as if he did. Mia was too angry and tired to think about the people's feelings. Yet there was one person who would have cared if he were there—Amir.

Amir's passionate words floated through Mia's thoughts, and while she remembered his words about people losing their life savings and their homes, it was Amir's look of sadness that struck a chord with Mia. It was his emotions that poured into Mia's words.

When Mia finished, she copied and pasted her words—Amir's words, as she thought of them—into an email. She sent that email to all major media outlets, and even the ones Amir was so fond of, before finally dragging herself to Calvin's bed. She didn't find Natasha there. Mia collapsed on the huge, lofty bed; the softness of the blankets didn't even register with her. She receded into the depths of Calvin's mind and fell asleep.

----

Mia was jolted awake by a screaming Natasha. "What did you do?" she was yelling.

Mia retreated to the back of James's mind, no longer controlling him.

"What are you talking about, woman?" James said, rolling over. He forced himself up and put a hand to his head.

"This!" Natasha shoved a tablet in front of James's face.

A news reporter showed an enlarged version of Mia's email to the viewers. She spoke about James Calvin's confession, and even how large sums of money had gone to the organizations that he allegedly stole money from.

"I did *what?*" James grabbed the tablet from his wife and stared at the screen.

"How much did you drink last night? You realize this is going to ruin us!" Natasha slapped James hard. Other than his head jerking, he didn't move in response.

"I-I…I don't remember," he said in a numb voice. "I-I…came home and—"

"And decided to destroy our lives," Natasha said coldly.

As fascinating as this all was, Mia felt as if she was intruding on a private moment between a husband and a wife. She knew that was ridiculous. Mia was the one who had caused it all in the first place. It was exactly what she had wanted. Yet now, all she wanted to do was go home to Amir and the comfort of his arms. She slipped from James to the maid. From the maid she slipped from body to body, heading to that crappy motel, and then back home.

# CHAPTER 4

**Mia had a huge** grin on her face when she arrived back at her apartment. In fact, she had one from the time she arrived back in her own body. The news everywhere was of James Calvin. She even heard people on the bus talking about what he'd done. She was curious as to what Calvin's next move would be, but that didn't matter now. What mattered was that her somewhat sloppy plan worked! The only question that occupied Mia's mind was, who was next? She'd have to be a little more meticulous in carrying out her plans, but to her mind, she was going to make sure that justice came due.

Amir came home with bags full of take-out food in his hands. "Hey," he said and kissed her. "How was your conference?"

"Boring, as always. Did anything interesting happen while I was gone?" She peered into the white, plastic bag. "Oooh, Indian. I'm starving."

"I don't know if you've heard the news, but James Calvin confessed. I told you it all works out in the end. He must have had a change of heart."

Mia said nothing, but gave Amir a smile. The innocent look on his face nearly broke her heart. She realized that she couldn't tell him what she'd done, nor what she planned to do. It would destroy the faith Amir had in the system and in his god.

----

The next morning, Mia overslept. Her body felt groggy, but she wasn't sick. Now that she was basking in the warmth of her success, she felt as if she could sleep for days. She vaguely remembered Amir waking her and asking if she was okay. Mia only mumbled in response. She got up and rubbed her forehead, wondering what was wrong with her, and then she remembered what she had done. Mia had pushed herself too hard over the weekend, using her powers to an extent that she wasn't prepared for. While she had grown into using her powers, she wasn't an expert. That would take time.

"I need to take it easy," Mia said.

She managed to drag herself out of bed and eat all of the Indian leftovers, not even thinking about the day's dinner. She needed the energy. She didn't work the rest of the day, instead just spending the day surfing the net, and watching TV shows while curled up in the couch. Why work anyway? She could afford to take the next few days off, especially with the money that James Calvin had provided.

Yet, it wasn't the money that caused Mia's dissatisfaction with her work. It was the feeling that her job wasn't fulfilling. Not that it had ever been fulfilling anyway, except to pay the rent, but her job meant far less to her now. With her newfound powers, she could do a lot more, and she could help people. It would seem like a waste to do nothing impactful with them.

The third day off work, Mia received a phone call that she couldn't ignore, unlike all the emails that she'd received. The company she worked for had summoned her into the office. As much as that annoyed her, she did feel like getting out of the house, and she was certainly better.

Mia enjoyed the bus ride downtown. Every time she was on this bus, she thought of Amir and how they first met. She missed those bus rides, and always tried to keep the seat next to her empty, as if he were there with her. But the empty seat couldn't replace leaning against him.

Mia was on time for her ten o'clock meeting, and that was the only professional thing about her. She wore a loose but comfortable black T-shirt, and leggings. Her unkempt hair was tied back and she wore no makeup. She sat down in the reception area until she was summoned.

Rebecca, Mia's boss, walked into the area. "Mia, hi! It's...good to see you again!" Rebecca's sharp green eyes weighed Mia. Mia knew it and didn't care. She had forgotten how unnaturally high Rebecca's voice sounded. It seemed to pierce through everything. "Come on in."

Mia followed Rebecca to her pristine and blindingly bright office. Much like her personality, everything about Rebecca was entirely too cheerful. Even the emails Mia received from her were too perky.

"I'm glad you could make it today," Rebecca said. "Since I hired you, I've known you to do nothing but exceptional work. That's one of the reasons why I've allowed you to work from home. But for the last week, your work has been...less than stellar. Bryan is concerned that he's been having to pick up the slack for you." Rebecca leaned forward and straightened her glasses. "Have you had some kind of problems at home?"

The look on Rebecca's face told Mia that she meant well, but Mia didn't care anymore. She didn't have time for these games, or even for worrying about things like jobs. She was meant for bigger things.

Mia reached across the desk and gently laid her hand on top of Rebecca's. "I'm sorry. Things have been tough for me lately. I *have* been going through some things. I promise you it will be different from now on."

Rebecca smiled and squeezed Mia's hand. "Glad to hear it. Just don't let it happen again."

When Mia pulled away from Rebecca, she let herself collapse into the office chair. She slipped into Rebecca's body, taking control of it. Mia tilted her head and watched her sleeping self. It didn't bother her as much as it used to. Mia closed the curtains before heading out of Rebecca's office.

Mia was so thankful to not have to work in an office anymore. She remembered feeling overjoyed with being able to telecommute, with the occasional in-person office meeting. If there was one thing that she'd learned over the years, it was that working in an office is like *The Office* without the sense of humor.

There was so much backstabbing, gossip, and food stealing that it was like being in high school. But at least in high school, you had the excuse of youth and hormones. There was no excuse here.

Most of the people on Mia's team could be counted on, but there was one who was always looking for an excuse to climb higher up the ranks by sticking his head up every butthole he could—Bryan.

Mia's anger rose as she stormed across the floor to where his—her—department was. She'd thought Bryan was a nice enough guy when she first met him, but she soon learned that despite the friendly smile and the apparent eagerness to help her, he was nothing but a backstabber. Mia shivered, remembering the one time when they had gone out. *To think that I actually let him kiss me.* Mia always had a feeling that Bryan resented her. She was better at their job than him. Despite being at the company a shorter time than him, she became lead and they let her telecommute from home.

When Mia walked into the department and into Bryan's own, smaller office, his face lit up with that cocky smile that made her want to punch him.

Bryan reached out to Mia, his hand tenderly holding hers. "Hey, babe. Is your meeting with Amelia already over? That was quick. I take it you were stern with her."

Mia's eyes widened and she gasped. She couldn't stop staring at Rebecca's and Bryan's hands. *They're a couple!* The revelation nearly made Mia burst out laughing. Luckily, she stifled it. What she couldn't control was the revulsion she felt in Rebecca's body as he held her hand.

Mia yanked her hand away. "I talked with…Mia today." Mia hated it when people used her full name. Made her feel like she was a kid again, and it always reminded her of her long-gone mother. It sounded worse coming from him. "Mia's had a rough time of it lately."

Bryan leaned forward, his eyes wide. "About what?"

Mia cracked her knuckles, feeling Rebecca's long fingernails dig into her hand. *I will not hit him. I will not hit him. I will not hit him.* "It's a personal matter. I shouldn't talk about it with you."

Bryan rose and smiled, inching closer to Mia. "I thought we were way past that."

She leaned back. "We are, but not at work. Mia's an excellent worker. She's great at her job. There's a reason why she was promoted over you."

Just as Mia suspected, those words did the trick. Bryan backed away from her and his shoulders slumped.

"I came here," Mia said, "to tell you to leave Mia alone. Her work may have been slipping as of late, but she does an excellent job."

"But—"

"Leave the poor woman alone. She got to her position because she's good at her job. I don't want you hassling her. It's not good for the company. Is that understood?"

Bryan's mouth was agape, but he nodded. "All right."

Mia could barely hear his voice, and that worried her. The pair must be more serious than she thought. While she was thankful not to have to be involved in office politics as much, a part of her missed the office gossip. That juicy drama could be more entertaining than any courtroom show. She headed for the door, wanting to get out of there as fast as possible. There was plenty of other work to do and she didn't want to be controlling Rebecca for too long.

"Oh God," Mia said, muttering under her breath. She rolled her eyes and paused at the door. Mia didn't want to ruin whatever it was they had together, even if it was Bryan. "I'll see you later!" She did her best to fake Rebecca's overly bright smile. When she did so, Bryan's face blossomed into a smile as well. Mia had to do her best to remember that he was looking at Rebecca, not her.

Mia hurried back to Rebecca's office. When she got there, she searched Rebecca's email. Just as she thought, there were a few emails detailing Mia's performance, including complaints from Bryan. Mia worked fast to mitigate the damage from those emails. By the time she was done, nearly an hour had passed. That was far longer than Mia wanted to be in Rebecca's body, but she had to make sure her job was assured...for now. She was already formulating ways to rob from the rich again and give to the poor, for a modest fee.

She slipped from Rebecca's body and back to her own.

Rebecca's face scrunched up in thought, and her mouth was open. She adjusted her glasses and said, "I'm sorry, I seem to have lost my train of thought."

Mia rose. "I've enjoyed our talk. We've been at it for over an hour."

"An hour?"

"I apologize again for my work. I promise you it won't happen again. And I trust you to be discreet with my...personal matters."

Rebecca cleared her throat and stood. "Yes, of course! Thank you for seeing me." A bright smile appeared on her face. "It was great to see you again!"

"It was great to see you too." The pair hugged. "We should catch up sometime."

"Yes, I would like that!"

"And maybe you can tell me about who you're now seeing."

A shocked expression crossed Rebecca's face. Mia couldn't help but smile as she exited the room. She knew the relationship between those two was secret. She hadn't seen any pictures of the other in either of their offices, and as annoyingly perky as Rebecca could be, Mia knew that she wouldn't want to flaunt their relationship or jeopardize her job because of Bryan.

With another victory under her belt, Mia returned home, feeling as if she could do anything, and that no one would be able to stop her.

----

Mia wished she could have told Amir about her day, but he would never understand. Instead, she would have to bask in triumph by herself. Later that night, Mia had a hard time sleeping. Even though she and Amir had quite the workout, she was feeling restless and wanted to go out into the city in someone's body. She thought about waking Amir, but decided against it. He needed his sleep for class tomorrow and as much as she wanted to, having sex with him again wouldn't be the best idea.

Instead, Mia decided to pay her favorite half-pint a visit. She slipped into Kate's body,

Mia found Kate at her computer like she normally did. When Mia got up and went to Ali's room, she expected to find the little girl in her bed, but she wasn't. Between Mia's plan for James Calvin and her job, she hadn't seen Ali as often as she would have liked. In fact, it had been over a week since she last saw Ali. Now that she thought about it, Mia never ran across Ali in the halls and Ali hadn't even come over for dinner that past Thursday.

When Mia checked Ali's room, she found it empty. Her bed was made, as if no one had been in it. Still, there was an unbearable, stale stench that crept into Mia's nose. She covered her nose and followed the smell, which led her to Ali's closet. An extension cord was tied around the handle and attached to the bed frame, to hold the door in place. Mia untied it and opened the closet door, and the smell grew stronger. She realized it was urine. As her eyes adjusted to the gloomy interior, Mia saw a figure at the bottom of the tiny closet, curled up into a ball—Ali.

Fear overtook Mia as she bent down to Ali's still body. The little girl's clothes were grimy and dirty and she reeked of urine and feces.

"Ali," Mia said softly, reaching out with her hand.

When Ali moved, Mia nearly jumped. "Mom...I'm sorry. Can I please come out now?" Ali struggled to open her eyes.

"What happened to you?" Mia asked.

Ali didn't seem to hear her. "I'm sorry. I'll never do it again. I promise. I'll be good, Mom. I'll be good."

"Shhh," Mia said, stroking Ali's matted hair. "Rest now."

Tears flowed from Mia as she carried Ali back to her bed. She called the ambulance and the police. While she waited for them, Mia knew that this was all her fault. She should have kept a closer eye on Kate. She should have intervened sooner. But no matter how bad a mother Kate was or how close Ali and Mia were, Mia didn't think a little girl should be without her mother. As much as Mia hated her mother for leaving her, she still wished that she had grown up with a mother.

When they arrived, Mia confessed to the police and once they had her in handcuffs and in the police car, she slipped out of Kate's body.

The next morning, Mia told Amir all about it.

"It's not your fault," Amir said as the pair sipped their coffee. "You didn't know Kate was doing this to Ali. A mother should not be like this."

Mia shook her head. "No, you were right. We should have called the authorities earlier. I couldn't be there all the time. I thought things were getting better." She sighed. "I was a fool."

Amir reached out and grabbed her hand. "We both were."

She allowed herself a small smile and squeezed his hand.

"I'm going to go visit her at the hospital and see how she's doing later today."

"Give her my best," Amir said. "I'll have to cook her favorite dish when she gets out."

Later that day, Mia went to the hospital and peeked inside Ali's room. It pained her to see the little girl hooked up to machines. Ali was watching her favorite cartoon, the one with the pink unicorn. Mia knew Ali loved that show, but the little girl didn't laugh out loud as she normally did when she watched it.

"Hey, half-pint," Mia said, walking in.

"Mia? Hi." Ali pulled her blankets up, trying her best to hide how terrible she looked.

Mia pulled up a seat and sat down next to the bed, gently placing her hand on Ali's leg. "It's all right. You don't need to be scared anymore, and you don't need to lie."

Ali pulled down her blankets and reached out for Mia's hand.

"I brought a book. It's another one of my favorites. It's called *Sideways Stories from Wayside School.* Would you like me to read it?"

Ali nodded.

----

Mia thought that with Kate out of the picture, things would start to get better for Ali. It was going to take time and Bill would have to man up and be a father, but time would heal Ali. Or at least that's what Mia believed.

A few days had passed and Ali finally returned home. Mia had been waiting for Ali, with a plate of Max's cookies. Unfortunately, Ali wasn't with her father. She was with Kate.

"What are you doing here?" Mia asked, eyeing her.

Kate returned the glare. "I'm bringing my daughter home. Why don't you stay inside and mind your own business?"

"I thought you got arrested."

Kate gasped. She paused before grabbing Ali's arm. "Come on, Ali. Let's go home."

Mia stepped in front of Kate, blocking her path. Something wasn't right. When Mia was in control of Kate, she'd confessed. They wouldn't have allowed her bail, and even if she'd gotten it, she shouldn't be allowed anywhere near Ali.

"Ali, where's your father?" Mia asked.

"He's—" When Ali glanced at Kate, her mother silenced her with a look.

"He won't be around much, not that it's any concern of yours," Kate said. She pushed Mia aside and yanked Ali with her.

As Ali glanced back at Mia, her eyes filled with sorrow and fear.

"And I want you to stay away from my daughter," Kate said, her voice like ice. "I mean it."

Mia felt helpless as she watched Ali and Kate disappear into their apartment. The door next to her cracked open.

"I never did like that woman," Max said, poking his head through the doorway. Once he saw Kate was gone, he opened his door all the way. "I've never seen someone with so much anger bottled up inside of them. And to think she has such a sweet little girl. Whatever's going on over there, I don't like it. I just wish there was something we could do about it." Max snatched one of his cookies from Mia's plate and went back inside.

But there was something Mia could do about it. She could make it so that Kate wouldn't be able to harm Ali ever again. But first, she had to find out what had happened to Bill.

# CHAPTER 5

**Mia slipped back** into Kate, not taking control of her, but merely observing.

"Go to your room," Kate said to Ali. "I don't want to see you again for the rest of the evening."

"OK, Mom," Ali said, heading into her room.

Kate took a handful of pills with her wine before sitting down on the couch. Mia watched as Kate drank more wine, while she pored over her emails and voice messages. Turned out Bill was the one who turned himself in. He confessed that it was him, not Kate, who had abused Ali. Mia couldn't believe that Bill would do such a thing, but he had. Now it looked like Kate would get off scot free and be without the husband who she clearly didn't love anymore, if she ever had.

As Kate took care of her business, Mia tried to think what to do about her. Without Bill, Kate would be even more of a monster. At least Bill tried to stem Kate, though he had failed at it. There had to be a way Mia could prove that Kate was the monster she was. She could do something in public, but Mia could never bring herself to harm Ali, even for a moment.

From the corner of Kate's eye, she saw Ali sneak out of her room. "What did I say?"

"I'm sorry, Mom. I had to go to the bathroom."

"Why doesn't anyone ever listen to me?" Kate slammed her laptop shut and stormed over to Ali.

Ali put her hands up, but it did her no good. Kate grabbed a handful of Ali's hair, dragging her back into the closet.

"No, Mom! Please! I didn't do anything."

"You never do," Kate said.

As Mia watched, she didn't understand how Kate could do such a thing or where all the rage she felt came from. All Mia knew was that Kate wouldn't stop. In that moment of clarity, Mia made her decision. A person couldn't change unless they *wanted* to change.

Mia took over Kate's body after she was done locking Ali in the closet. It was best if Ali wasn't there to witness what Mia had planned.

Mia had to hurry. It wouldn't be long before Amir got home. He would try to stop her, and she knew she would stop if he asked.

As Mia sat down at Kate's table, doing her best not to run into Ali's room and release her, she thought of her own mother's death.

*What would Kate write?* Mia asked herself as she stared at the blank piece of paper on the table. She wouldn't write a letter, for one thing. Mia had gotten to know Kate well, and she knew that for a fact. Yet the letter she was supposed to write had to not only read that Kate was responsible for the abuse, but to bare Kate's feelings and her soul. It had to be moving and tearful.

Mia glanced up at the ceiling, and then an inspiration came to her. "Thank you, Mother."

Tears fell from Mia's eyes as she remembered the letter her own mother had left. She hadn't thought about it in years. Once she started, she couldn't stop sobbing. A little girl shouldn't be without a mother, but no matter how bad Mia's own mother got or what kind of issues she had, she never abused her own daughter. She never made Mia feel afraid of her, but she did make Mia feel afraid *for* her. What Mia was doing was a gamble, but Ali needed to be away from Kate and never fear her own mother again. Ali's father was going to have to step up and be a man. If he didn't, then Mia would handle him next and take care of Ali herself.

All of the pent-up emotion Mia had repressed over the years poured into that letter. She had told Amir what happened to her mother, but hadn't gone into detail. That detail was now in this letter, but with Kate's touch to it. How sorry she was for what she had done to Ali and Bill, and how she forced him to take the blame for her. How frustrating and high-pressure her job was, and that she wrongfully took it out on her family. That she never meant to do it, but the rage boiled over and she just did.

Mia wrote that Ali would be better off without her. That she had such a bright future and that if Kate stayed around, she would destroy that future. Ali needed a positive influence in her life.

The letter was stained with Mia's tears. Those would add to the authenticity. She put the letter down and checked Kate's computer one final time. Just as she thought, there was a sizable life insurance policy through Kate's company. Ali would be well taken care of financially. Mia left the apartment and headed to the roof.

The biting wind made Mia shiver, and she had to shield her eyes from the glaring sun. Mia stood on the roof's edge, peering down into the abyss. *It's a long way down,* she thought. Doing it this way was cleaner than a gun, and gave her plenty of opportunity to slip out of Kate's body. Still, she had never tried anything like this. Mia wasn't sure if she could slip out from Kate's body in time. But images of Ali's pale body, lying trapped in the closet, haunted Mia. With that on her mind, she took one step off the roof.

Mia felt the sudden drop in the pit of her stomach, like being on a roller coaster. Now, for the other reason why she'd chosen the roof as her method. It took time—time for Kate to realize what was happening. She receded back into Kate's mind, giving her back control of her body.

Kate blinked, bewildered as she felt the wind flapping hard against her face. Confused and terrified, she prayed it was a dream. She was just in her apartment with Ali. But the cold air whipping against her cheeks and the relentless pull of gravity told her otherwise. Kate gave a bloodcurdling scream as she plummeted to her doom.

*Good,* Mia thought. *This is for Ali.*

Mia didn't want to know what would happen to her if Kate died while Mia was inside her. Mia tried slipping out of Kate's body, but each time she felt someone on one of the building's floors, they passed by too quickly. Mia just couldn't latch on to them.

It was all going by so fast and Mia had a hard time focusing. *I have to concentrate.* Mia reached out with her mind, feeling her powers strain against Kate's body and gravity.

*There!* Before Kate's body slammed into the ground, Mia left. Her essence was pulled into a slumbering body hidden under pieces of ratty cardboard. The impact of Kate's body jolted him awake, but soon he was no longer in control.

Mia broke out in laughter. It had worked! Then she started coughing uncontrollably. The body she was in clearly wasn't healthy, but that didn't matter now. What mattered was that Ali would no longer have to put up with Kate's abuse.

Tears welled up in Mia as she remembered what it was like to not have a mother. It was going to be hard for Ali, but Mia would be there for her.

Mia slipped from the homeless man's body and began the journey back to her apartment.

----

After Mia returned to her body, the worst part was the waiting. It would take some time before the police came, and even more until they identified Kate. They would then go over to Kate's apartment. What Mia wanted to do was run over to their apartment and free Ali from her prison, hugging her tightly and telling her that everything was going to be OK now. But she didn't dare. The police would ask too many questions. They were going to ask questions anyway, but it was best if they didn't ask the right ones.

Time passed and eventually the police arrived at Ali's place. Not long after, Amir came home.

"Beloved," he said, walking through the door. "You should see this. Something's going on at Ali's. I wonder—" He stopped, seeing the look on Mia's face. He knew something was wrong. "What is it?"

"I…I have something to tell you."

Mia told the story of what had happened when Kate and Ali returned home, and how she was responsible for Kate's death.

When Mia was finished, Amir couldn't bear to look at her. She reached out to touch his hand and Amir yanked it away. He stood up and began pacing around the room. Thoughts raced through his head—about his beloved, his Mia.

Amir needed something to drink. His eyes wandered to the cabinet where they kept a couple of bottles of liquor to entertain company with. He hadn't had a drink in years, but he was almost tempted to start again.

He went to the fridge instead, and downed a bottle of water to soothe his dry throat. When he closed the refrigerator door, his eyes focused on the picture stuck to the door with a magnet. It was of him and Mia, taken a long time ago. They were on their third date, on the pier at the fair. Both of them had colorful balloon shapes on their heads. They looked ridiculous but it was on that day that Amir realized he loved her.

What had happened to that Mia?

"Amir," Mia said, approaching him carefully. "Please say something."

He sighed. "What do you want me to say?" His gaze finally met hers. "How could you take her life? What were you thinking? You *murdered* Ali's mother!"

"Shhhh. Will you keep your voice down? The police are still outside."

Amir cracked his knuckles, his body aching for something to numb the pain he felt. He glanced back at the picture on the fridge before staring at the woman in front of him. His beloved had changed. The woman he looked at now wasn't the one he had fallen in love with.

"Because of you, Ali's going to grow up without a mother," Amir said. "No child should have to go through that."

Mia threw her hands up in frustration. "Don't you think *I* of all people know that?" Tears flooded Mia's eyes. "There's not a day that goes by that I don't miss my mother! But she was unwell. If she'd stayed in my life, she would have destroyed me."

"No," Amir said, his voice firm. "Your mother killed herself. *You* killed Ali's mother. You took the choice out of both Ali's and Kate's hands."

"You weren't there. You didn't see what I saw. Ali looked like she was at death's door in that closet, and Kate threw her back in. She was in there for days the last time. How long was Kate going to keep her in this time? Until she died? I wasn't going to let that happen."

Amir watched the righteousness and superiority melt away from Mia. Through her tears, he saw how fearful and unsure she looked. Yet through all that, he saw how much she cared, how much she loved Ali, and how damaged she was by her own mother. God help him. He still loved her, and he saw his old Mia there, standing vulnerable in spite of her power. Despite all the wrong Mia had done, Amir believed that he saw how sorry Mia was for killing Kate.

Yet as much as Amir loved Mia, this would be the one thing he would never forget. He would always know that she had taken a life. Amir sighed and put his hand to his head. He loved Mia more than he had thought possible, but he now felt responsible for her as well. She was dangerous, and he would have to remember that.

Mia always thought Amir's compassion was one of his more endearing qualities, but after the things she had seen, she now thought it made him a little weak and soft-hearted as well. She also knew that Kate's death would be the one issue they would never get over. Yet Amir wasn't the one with this power—Mia was. She could make the hard choices Amir couldn't. Mia did what had to be done. She wasn't going to let Kate harm Ali anymore.

There were other things she had done, too. Mia bit her lip, debating whether or not to tell Amir about them. This would be the time to tell him. *Good relationships are built on trust and honesty,* she thought. Bad ones…well, she had had plenty of bad ones to draw experience from. There was also another reason she didn't want to tell Amir. He would be an accessory to what she had done. But he would want to know, and he would begin to hate her if she didn't tell him.

"There's more," Mia said and bit her lip.

"More?"

She nodded, and began telling the rest of her story about what she'd done to James Calvin, and even what she'd done to her boss.

When she was finished, Amir turned his back to her and walked towards the window. He saw her reflection in the glass. It was almost as if a stranger stared back at him.

"Why?" Amir asked. "Why did you do such things?"

Mia crept up to Amir, aching for him to hold her and tell her that everything would be all right. But it wouldn't be. Things would be different now, she knew, and she feared losing him more than anything else.

"I did what I did because both Calvin and Kate deserved to have something happen to them. Ali and the people deserved justice. They couldn't be allowed to do whatever they want."

"Like you."

Mia froze, never having heard such a cold voice from Amir. "But I'm nothing like them. I haven't used my powers to hurt people."

"What about Rebecca?"

Rebecca had nothing to do with it, but then Mia realized that was the point. She had used her power for personal gain and slacked off work because of it. Past conversations with Amir floated through her mind. He always believed that things didn't start out bad. That people had good intentions and often started small before spiraling out of control. *Was that what I was doing?*

"What do you want me to do?" she asked.

Amir finally turned around and faced her. He considered his words and softened his voice, much like he would to a troubled child in his classroom, or a dangerous and deadly animal. *Is that how I think of her now?* Amir thought. Yet he knew that he was the only one who could reason with her. And despite all she'd done, God help him, he loved her and he always would.

"Beloved," he said, "I want you to be careful and please stop all of this."

"But I have these powers. You're the one who says that if you have the power you should *do* something with it."

"Something *responsible* with it."

Mia was silent as she thought about the future. The world was open to her now. She could do anything she put her mind to. After all, who could possibly stop her?

Amir reached up with a tender hand and placed it against her face. "I fear for you, beloved. You ruined a man's life, toyed with a friend,      and      murdered      someone. You're…changing."

The world might have been open to Mia, but the door to Amir was beginning to close.

Mia stepped forward, closing the gulf between them. She was thankful and relieved when Amir opened his arms to accept her. Mia sobbed, collapsing onto his chest. She didn't want to lose him.

"I'm sorry," Mia said. "I'll stop until we can think of more responsible things to do with my powers."

Amir squeezed her tighter. "We'll do this together, like we've always done." Still, as much as Amir loved Mia, he couldn't get her selfish deeds out of his mind. But he would help her atone for her sins and be there for her like he always was. A thought whispered in the back of his mind that one day, she might go too far. Where would they be then?

There was a knock at the door. It wasn't the familiar sound of any one of their neighbors. They knew who it was—the police.

# CHAPTER 6

**Over the next** few days, Mia struggled to heed Amir's words. As much as she wanted to, she didn't use her powers. They still hadn't decided on what she should do with them. They settled back into their routine, and she tried to focus on her work, but it was hard for her. She had gotten used to her powers, and using them had become second nature to her. She didn't want to lose Amir, but she didn't want to deny who she now was. Mia didn't admit it to herself, but she began to resent Amir.

After staring at code for a couple of hours, Mia took a break from working and walked to the local coffee shop. It was entirely too cold to be out, but that's why she—and everyone else—was buying coffee on this chilly day. She needed to get away and think.

"This isn't what I ordered," a man at the front of the line said loudly.

Mia leaned to the side and spotted the man. He was young with slicked-back hair, and his well-pressed suit must have cost a bundle. He had a death grip on his phone, and he was constantly exaggerating his expressions.

"How hard is it to get a coffee order right?" he asked, his free hand going to his forehead. "It's not rocket science, for God's sake. It's *coffee*."

"I know, sir," the kid behind the counter said. "I'm sorry, but—"

The man flicked his wrist, his manicured nails shining bright to Mia. "I asked for my latte to be *light* on the milk and have caramel drizzle on top of the con panna, not under it."

"Excuse me, sir," a slightly older woman than the cashier said. Her freckles made her look younger, though. "I'm the manager. If you'd please—"

The man gave an exasperated sigh. "Manager? You're barely out of grade school. In fact—"

Mia put her fingers to her temples, trying to drown out the obnoxious man's voice. His high-pitched whining smashed through Mia's patience. She left the line and sat down in the nearest free chair.

*Enough!* her mind screamed as she slipped from her own body and into his. When Mia took over his body, she forced the man to stop his incessant whining.

"I want to apologize," Mia said from inside the man's body, loud enough for everyone to hear. Everyone turned to look her way. "It's been a stressful week, at work and in my personal life, so I must have let it get the best of me."

Mia pulled out his wallet and swept his arms in a grand motion, as she was sure he'd do. "To make up for me being such an ass, I will pay for everyone's coffee." Mia pulled out his credit card. "And free scones and muffins or whatever else you want too!"

Everyone in the shop cheered. Mia hurried and paid for everything. Mia walked past herself and went outside with coffee in hand. As soon as she reached the limits of her powers, she slipped back into her body and left the bewildered man.

"Are you all right, miss?" the young manager asked.

Mia blinked, surprised that the manager had come over to her. "I'm fine, thank you. Sorry, I suffer from a condition if I have a lack of sugar. It's why I sat down—why I came in here in the first place."

The young woman grinned. "That rude man offered to buy coffee for everyone in here, and a small snack."

Mia smiled. "Oh, he did?"

She nodded. "Yes, now what can I get you?"

Eventually, Mia got her order and sat at a table with a chocolate muffin and warm milk in hand. It wasn't what she originally came to order, but she never could resist a free muffin, even if she had made the guy buy it for her. As she chewed the delicious muffin, she realized that what she had done made her feel good. That man deserved what he got, and if his credit card bill was a little higher, then so be it.

It was at that moment that Mia realized that as much as she loved Amir and didn't want to lose him, he wasn't going to stop her from using her talent. He just didn't have to know about it.

Mia decided to take a bus ride, even though she had walked to the coffee shop. It relaxed her, and she wished that Amir was there even if she couldn't tell him what she planned to do. *And where to strike first?* Mia thought.

The world was open to her now. She exhaled, listening to the people around her. A college-aged couple behind her argued about all the police brutality that was happening in what seemed like every major city. An elderly man was on the phone talking about how he was going to manage since the government cut his payments again. A young teenager in a fast food uniform told his girlfriend that he wished he could spend more time with her and their young baby, but he had to go to his second job.

*There's so much wrong with the world,* she thought. She might not be able to fix it all, but she could do something.

"Like a superhero," Mia said to herself, grinning.

----

Over the next two weeks, Mia pushed herself to the edge. She still had a job to do and was a surrogate mother to Ali and a loving girlfriend to Amir, but when they were asleep, she had her own life.

In her double life, Mia slipped into other people's bodies, and she loved being free again. At first, she would only go into cops or emergency medical technicians. People she thought would need the most help, and where she would catch the most action. But those overnight shifts were boring. There was a lot of waiting. She needed to be out in the streets.

It wasn't long before Mia rode inside of other people's bodies, traversing the night. She stopped simple things like a pimp slapping a hooker, a man getting mugged, or a druggie about to break a car window. While stopping those crimes bolstered Mia's confidence, it didn't feel like it was enough. When she had ruined James Calvin, it impacted far more people. With her powers, she could and should do more.

That's when Mia realized that comic book superheroes had been doing it wrong. Instead of attacking the symptoms, they should have attacked the source. She had the power to bring it all down, and that's what she was going to do.

----

Amir was having a hard time sleeping. He tossed and turned until he woke up, turning to Mia. He saw her sleeping, peaceful face and smiled. He realized how lucky he was to have found a woman like her. The thing he loved most about her was that she made him feel like he was always at home when he was around her. Instead of a stranger in this land. His mother had never cared much for American girls, but he wished that she would stop her old-fashioned way of thinking and just give Mia a chance. His mother could be so stubborn sometimes, and she didn't realize that she and Mia were more alike than either of them thought.

As Amir stared at her, he still couldn't believe the things she could do. Her gifts were what kept him up at night. He was so worried for her and for what the future could hold. Another reason he loved her was that she could do anything when she put her mind to it. Her passionate drive made her irresistible to him. No doors were closed to her now. The only thing that could hold her back...

*Is me,* Amir thought. That thought scared him. He didn't want to control or manipulate her, yet he also didn't want her being reckless, ruining people's lives, or worse yet, killing people. Kate was a terrible person and an even worse mother and she deserved punishment, but it wasn't up to him or Mia to decide what that was. Amir needed to think of something to help Mia. What bothered him most was that her abilities were putting the plans he had for them on hold.

But all of those worries could wait. It had been awhile since either of them had woken up in the middle of the night and made passionate love to the other. Amir began kissing Mia, and then caressing her with his hands. He paused when she didn't respond. It took some doing, depending on how tired she was, but he was always able to rouse her from her sleep.

"Beloved," Amir said. "Beloved," he repeated, louder. He shook her but she didn't move, no matter how hard he tried. Panic overtook Amir. He got up, reaching for his phone to call to call 911. Then he remembered what happened to Mia whenever she used her powers, and put his phone down.

Amir leaned closer and opened up Mia's eyelids, seeing her lifeless eyes staring back at him. He sighed. "Where are you and what are you doing?"

Sleep eluded Amir that night as he watched over her, worried. What was she was doing? Was she all right? If she got hurt or even killed in another's body, what would happen to her soul?

Eventually, Amir did nod off, but the alarm jolted him awake a moment later. He groaned, thinking he had just fallen asleep, but he dragged himself out of bed and into his morning routine. As the hot shower struck Amir's face, he couldn't help but think of Mia. He needed to talk to her about all this, but he didn't know when a good time would be, or how to confront her. He breathed a little easier when he went back to the bedroom and saw that she was up.

*Maybe she was just having a night on the town.* Amir would give it a few days, maybe even a week or two. For all he knew, she just needed to get it out of her system. He would stand by her and pray that's all it was.

"How are you?" Amir asked as he sipped his morning cup of coffee.

Mia paused from drinking her own coffee and looked at him. "I'm fine. Why do you ask?"

"I just wanted to know if you had any more bad dreams."

She shook her head. "I haven't had any of them in awhile."

"Glad to hear it. Wouldn't want you to get any more strange powers, like sprouting horns from your head." He smiled and she returned it.

A look of concern passed over Mia's face. "What's wrong?"

Amir yawned. "Just tired. I barely got any sleep last night."

Mia walked over until her body was leaning into Amir's. "I hope you're not too tired."

He leaned down with a sly smile on his face. "Oh, what for?"

She grinned, then kissed him. "You'll see."

They had a great evening that night and she did her best to please him, but Mia suspected that Amir knew something. There was just something off about the way he acted. But then again, it might be her guilt. Mia didn't feel guilty about what she was doing but about the fact that she was hiding it from Amir. Normally, they could tell each other anything.

A month passed and Amir never gathered up the courage to confront Mia about her activities. He was a coward, he knew. But he was also afraid of what she would say, and what it would mean for their relationship and the future.

Amir sat on the couch, trying to come up with the next week's lesson plan. It was a challenge being a teacher. Sure, he could use the same lesson plan year after year—it's not like the kids would know the difference. But what he thought made a good teacher, was someone who worked with the kids, and kept them engaged and challenged them. Though doing so, did make his job a little harder. But he wouldn't change it for anything in the world.

The news was on in the background, as it usually was when Amir worked. Mia was curled up on the couch with her tablet, her feet on his lap, watching whatever show with a love triangle that she adored. Amir wasn't watching the news, but he was hearing it.

A medical company worth billions was giving away a very expensive drug. Free clinics all over the city were inviting people come in to get their shot. Amir stopped his work and started paying attention to the news. He smiled, glad that the company was doing some good. From what he knew, they had been accused of raising prices above what many who needed the drug could afford.

Amir reached for his glass of water. From the corner of his eye, he caught the expression on Mia's face. Her eyes were glued to the television set, which they never were when the news was on. She always found the news just as boring as he found most of the shows she watched. Yet when he saw how intent her eyes were and how she had a little smile curling her mouth, he knew the truth.

"Were you responsible for this?" Amir asked. He tried, but he couldn't keep the accusation out of his voice.

Mia paused before setting her tablet on her lap. "I was."

Amir exhaled and put his palm to his head. He tried to find words, but he didn't have anything.

Mia forced herself up from her comfortable position. "Come on, say something."

"I don't know what to say. I thought we agreed that you wouldn't do anything until we could figure out how you can use your powers constructively."

"I was wrong to agree to it. Clearly, you haven't thought of anything, and were buying time."

The lovers glared at each other and said nothing.

"And this is how you've spent your nights?" Amir asked. "Planning to ruin a company?"

"*Ruin?* I'm trying to help people." She tossed aside her tablet, standing and pointing. "It's what *you've* always said and wanted."

Amir rose and in a soft voice said, "I get that, and I love you for it. But you shouldn't be judge, jury, and executioner. There's no balance to it. Your heart's in the right place, but that's too much power even for you. Can't you see what this is doing to you?"

"I'm not going to let you control me and run my life. I'm going to do what I want. These powers are a part of me now. You're going to have to learn to accept it."

Amir's shoulders slumped, and he grabbed his coat and walked to the door. He opened the door and paused, not quite able to meet her gaze. Finally, he lifted his head and looked into her eyes. "I never wanted to control you, beloved."

Amir left their apartment, walking the neighborhood with no purpose. The drop in temperature got to him and he eventually found himself in a dive bar. He was never one for bars now, but in his youth, he had known a few. Far too many of today's bars were brightly lit and clean, full of kids in their early twenties.

"When did I get so old?" he asked, stepping inside. Amir was fast approaching thirty.

Three older men turned to look at Amir as he let his eyes adjust to the dim lighting. There were only a handful of people at the bar and they all clearly wanted to be left alone—it was just what Amir wanted. When he seated himself at the bar, he ordered a shot and downed it. The bitter alcohol burned his throat, but he asked for another. The second one he took his time with, but it wasn't long before there was a third and a fourth.

As Amir drank, he tried to figure out when the power Mia now wielded had started corrupting her. A small part of him began to wonder if she wasn't always like that. He shook his head, trying to clear his thoughts. No, the power might have brought out the worst in Mia, but she was still the woman he loved. There had to be a way they could get through this. He didn't want to lose her, but he also didn't want her to do more harm.

"Hey, handsome," said an older but attractive woman, dressed in a black business suit. She sat on the stool next to Amir. "Buy you a drink?"

*Where had she come from, and what was she doing in a place like this?* "Thank you for the offer, but I'm taken."

The woman laughed in delight. "If I were ten years younger, maybe. Bartender, two beers please. You, my friend, need something lighter."

After the drinks arrived, she held out her glass and Amir clinked his to hers. "Thank you for the beer."

"Any time." She swallowed a gulp of beer. "Women troubles?"

"How did you know?"

"It's always women troubles with you men."

Amir took a sip, then shrugged. He cleared his throat and said, "This isn't like anything you've ever heard of."

She raised an eyebrow. "Try me."

He turned to look at her. It might have been the liquor, but he thought about telling this woman—this stranger—the things Mia could do. He shook his head, deciding against it. No matter how drunk Amir was, he wouldn't betray Mia's trust. Besides, this woman would just think he was crazy.

Amir finished the drink. "Thank you for the beer, but I've got to be going. It's getting late."

"Wait." The woman grabbed his arm. Either Amir had drunk way too much, or the woman was a lot stronger than she looked. "Ms. Olsen—Ameila—needs help."

He tightened up, wanting to tear his arm from her grasp. How did she know Mia's name? But he had to know if what she said was true. "What do you mean?"

She let go of his arm and grabbed her beer, pausing before she drank. "You think Amelia is the only one with...abilities?" She took another swig of beer.

Amir's eyes widened and he sat back down, using the bar to steady himself. There were *more* people like Mia? Of course there were others. She couldn't possibly be the only one. The world was too big a place and there were far too many people.

A sly smile spread across the woman's face. "You have no idea of the world you've stepped into, Mr. Fawzi."

"What—what other kind of people are there?"

"That's above your pay grade. What is important is that we can help Amelia. We've encountered two others with her ghosting ability."

"Ghosting?" Amir asked. "Is that what it's called?"

"It's a term a couple of my colleagues came up with. I don't much care for it, as it's highly inaccurate, but it's stuck." The levity in the woman's voice disappeared along with her smile. "Amelia has powers she doesn't understand. She needs to learn to control her powers, and to not interfere in things that don't concern her."

Amir's hand tightened around the glass bottle. "How did you find her?"

"That bit with the drug company brought her to our attention. We've looked into her past and have noticed that as of late, strange events have been occurring around her. A neighbor commits suicide and a successful businessman has a change of heart. Very interesting events indeed. Who knows what else she will do if left unchecked?"

Amir stared into the empty beer bottle. He swirled the remaining droplets, wishing he had another drink. The thought of ordering another, much stronger drink occurred to him, but no, he needed to be clearheaded for what came next. Well, as clear-headed as his already alcohol-soaked brain could manage.

He didn't look at the woman. "I don't even know who you are."

She stuck out her hand. "My name is Zelda, Amir. A pleasure to meet you."

# CHAPTER 7

**The next couple** of days were tense between Amir and Mia. They had had fights before, but never one that lasted this long. Even Ali knew something was wrong, and she never stayed at their apartment for very long. They still went through their routine, but fewer pleasantries were said. They only spoke when they had to. Mia no longer made coffee for them in the morning, and Amir stopped cooking.

They had entirely too much pride to say that they were both miserable without the other.

One evening, Amir stopped working on his lesson plan for the next day and went to the bedroom where Mia was. She pretended to bury her attention in her tablet, but she knew he was there.

"Hey," Amir said, sitting down. He fidgeted with the blankets and couldn't quite look her in the eyes. "Would you like to go out tonight and ride the bus?"

Mia was still angry at Amir, but ever since their fight, even though she had ghosted she hadn't taken matters into her own hands in any situation. She turned to look at Amir, her angry eyes softening. "I'd like that."

Later that evening, they grabbed their coats and ventured into the chilly night. They walked in tune with each other, but still left a gap of space between them without a word said. When they got on the bus, only ten passengers were onboard. It was late and well past rush hour. They sat in the exact seats where they first met, with Mia taking the window seat. They rode in silence, watching the people get on and off the bus and glancing at the changing view outside the window.

An hour passed with them not speaking. Soon, Mia leaned against Amir, her body fitting perfectly with his.

"I missed this," she said. "And I've missed you."

"Me too," he said, wrapping his arm around her. "I'm sorry."

As Amir and Mia whispered their private conversation, they became oblivious to the world around them, not realizing where the bus was taking them. They poured their feelings out to each other, and they remembered how well they connected with one another. Their conversation went on so long that nearly all the bus passengers had gotten off. There were only two others left.

"All right," Mia said, looking up at Amir. "I'll tone it down. But I still want to help people. Maybe you can finally help me come up with some ideas."

He smiled. "I'll try. I don't want you to be ghosting into something dangerous."

"Ghosting?" Mia had a quizzical expression on her face. "Where did you come up with that?"

Amir opened his mouth, but before he could answer, she interrupted him.

Mia was staring out the window. The buildings and lights of the city had vanished. They were outside the city now. "Does this bus have a different route now? I don't remember this."

The two passengers left rose. The one in front said nothing, but the one behind her spoke.

"Good evening, Ms. Olsen. A pleasure to meet you."

Mia stood, and so did Amir. "Do I know you?" Mia asked, narrowing her eyes at the stranger.

"No, but Mr. Fawzi does."

When Amir clenched his fist and bit the inside of this cheek, Mia knew there was far more that he hadn't told her.

"I'm sorry, Mia," Amir said. "Zelda approached me a few nights ago when I was drinking, and she *knew* about you." He could barely meet Mia's eyes. "I thought she could help you."

"You mean *control* me."

"He means help you," Zelda said, taking a step forward. So did the man at the other end. "We can help you understand your powers if you'll work with us."

"You mean *for* you."

"The world's bigger than you know. You're only now stepping into it. You'll need help navigating it."

"I was doing just fine on my own, thank you."

Zelda crept closer, using the bus handles to steady herself. "Creating chaos is more like it."

Mia glanced at the man behind her, noticing a bulk underneath his suit jacket. She had no doubt that the woman also carried a weapon. "And what will you do if I say no?"

"Amelia, this is ending, one way or another. I would prefer you to come with us willingly. Even in his drunken state Amir spoke very highly of you. I could see it in his eyes. The young man loves you more than the world itself."

Mia's eyes softened when she looked at Amir. Poor, gullible Amir. She grabbed his arm and smiled up at him. He always saw the good in people and tried to do the right thing. But there were people in this world that would take advantage of his good-natured naivety. This Zelda was one of them.

"I assume you've read up on me and studied me," Mia said, her fierce gaze meeting Zelda's eyes.

She nodded. "I have."

"Then you already know my answer."

"Unfortunately, I do. But Amir had given me hope for another."

"Mia, what are you doing?" Amir asked, feeling the sweat on his hands. "You've got to hear them out. She said there are others like you. They could help you. Give them a chance."

"Why? They didn't give me one." There was an edge of steel in her voice. "There was a reason why they wanted you to bring me on this bus—*our* bus. They knew I would come and they knew that if that happened, they could get me away from people I could…ghost into."

Amir's mouth opened as he turned to Zelda. He almost asked the question, but when he saw Zelda's cold eyes, hidden behind a warm, false smile, he knew Mia's words to be true. "No. What do you plan to do to her?"

"Don't worry," Mia said. "I won't let it happen."

With the practice Mia had been doing, she was a lot faster in using her powers. She knew she could ghost into their bodies and take away their weapons in the blink of an eye. Mia's soul sprinted towards Zelda, but the moment she did, her essence was flung back into her own body.

"Ahhhh!" Mia screamed.

Amir caught her and glared at Zelda. "What did you do to her?"

"Nothing. She did it to herself." She pushed aside her hair and revealed a device that looked like a hearing aid. Blue lights emanated from it, lighting up before dulling again. "Interesting devices we had to come up with. They stop people like Mia from getting into places where they don't belong."

Amir laid Mia on the bus seat, as she still needed time to recover. Whatever those devices were, they did more than keep someone from ghosting into the wearer. They hurt.

"So what now?" Amir asked. "You're going to kill us."

Zelda frowned. "Mr. Fawzi, please. We're not monsters. We would prefer to do this the easy way. If you come with us, Ms. Olsen, we can remove your ability to ghost and you can go back to your normal life and loving boyfriend. If not, there are more...extreme measures we will take."

"But...," Mia said in a barely audible voice. "It's a...part of me."

"I was afraid you'd say that," Zelda said. "They all do. Yet the threat does need to be neutralized."

Zelda and her associates reached into their pockets. They plugged their noses, and the bus driver flipped a switch that caused gas to pour out from the bus's air-conditioning system.

Amir poised himself to move, but Zelda pulled out her gun. "Mr. Fawzi, I would hate to have to shoot you."

The gas began to seep into their mouths and noses. Amir coughed, and so did Mia. He had to do something. All of this was his fault. He gripped one of the bus's poles, trying not to fall over. When he looked to Mia, he saw how heavy her eyes were. The gas affected Mia far worse than Amir. He thought it might be because he was bigger than her, but then realized that wasn't it. The gas must be specially formulated to affect people like Mia. No matter how groggy and sluggish Mia became, she kept fighting. But Amir could see that it was a losing battle.

He stared at Mia, then at the gun Zelda had pointed at him, feeling the effects of the gas start to overtake him. He let out a silent prayer to Allah to give him strength to do what was needed. No matter what happened to him, he wasn't going to let them take or kill his beloved.

Out of all the people in the world, Amir was one of the more peaceful ones. He rarely raised his voice, and he had never gotten into a fight in his adult years. There was a calm aura about him. That aura had attracted Mia to him, as she had dated far too many men who were nothing like that. Yet those calm people always had this inner rage that threatened to come out whenever someone they loved was in harm's way. Like now.

Amir roared and rushed Zelda. Zelda was surprised, as she didn't think Amir was capable of such a thing. She barely had time to level her gun, firing it at Amir. The bullet pierced him, but didn't slow him down. His concern for Mia and the guilt Amir felt fueled his body as he tackled Zelda.

Amir didn't want to hit Zelda, but he had to get that gun away from her. He was stronger than she was and he had caught her off guard, but she was trained and knew how to maneuver her body so that he couldn't get a solid grip on it.

A second gun fired from behind Amir. He loosened his grip on Zelda and her gun, collapsing on her.

"Amir!" Mia screamed, not caring that more gas got in her mouth. She struggled to rise, but with each breath, her body grew heavier. If she was to die, she wanted to lie in his arms one last time.

Zelda climbed out from under Amir. She gave a look to her partner, and he lowered his gun. "Ms. Olsen, I wish it hadn't come to this. I liked Amir. He was a good man and a good teacher. In my line of work and experience, both are extremely hard to come by."

"No." A weak voice struggled to speak. It was Amir. He had gotten Zelda's gun and now leveled it at her.

Zelda frowned, but she didn't move. "You're not going to kill me, Mr. Fawzi. I know killers, and you're not one."

"You're...right," Amir said, pointing the gun at Mia.

Mia gasped and flinched as Amir fired the gun. The bullet sailed over her head, crashing into the bus's window and shattering it. The gas flooded out the window.

"Run!" Amir yelled.

When Amir's strength failed him and he dropped the gun, Mia hesitated. She ached to reach out to him and save him. But Zelda's associate was already aiming his gun at her.

"Run, beloved," Amir said, coughing up blood. "Run..."

Mia staggered away from everyone, heading towards the broken window. She tried to leap through it, but instead fell through the hole. The glass tore into her and her body fell heavily onto the street. She yelled in pain, feeling an arm and a leg break.

Zelda took the gun from Amir and said, "There was a time when I would have done anything for love."

"No," Amir said, reaching out to grab her before his arm gave way.

"I'm sorry, Mr. Fawzi. I truly am. There's only one way this can now end. Though I suppose I always knew it would." Zelda walked to the back of the bus, seeing Mia's figure crawling on the dark road. "Stop the bus." She peered out the window, judging the distance. "Back it up and stay as straight as you can."

Thoughts of Amir filled Mia's head, pushing out the pain. He was dead, and all she could think of was how stupid she'd been the last few days. If only she had had one more delicious dinner of his, if only she had had one more piggyback ride as he climbed up the stairs in laughter, if only she had had one more night in bed with him inside her, beside her and intertwined with her. If only…

But Mia couldn't think of such things now. She pushed aside the tears and tried to crawl, but her broken, bloodied body wouldn't let her. Every muscle and bone cried out. The bus's reverse lights came into view. Mia had to get out of there fast, but try as she might, she could only move an inch or two. The pain wracked her body and it wouldn't obey her.

Mia reached out with her ability. The agents, as she thought of them, had chosen their location well. There was no one around them on the lonely road. She easily felt the agents, but she wasn't going to try to ghost into them again. Her heart lightened when she realized that Amir was alive. But that energy that Mia sensed within him was fading fast. She knew she could ghost into him, but what would happen if he died while she was still inside him?

Mia still held out hope for her love. She genuinely believed that Zelda liked Amir. She might even try to save him once she was done with Mia. Mia couldn't be sure what would happen to Amir if he survived his wounds, but she couldn't enter him. She wouldn't risk it. Zelda might shoot Amir just to stop her, if she knew Mia was in there. There had to be another way.

The cold helped numb Mia's body, or maybe shock was setting in from all the injuries she had suffered, but either way, it helped her to concentrate.

"There," she said, weakly. She felt a flicker of life off in the distance. Maybe it was a bicyclist, maybe it was a stranded driver, or just a passing car. Whomever it was, Mia didn't care. All she cared about was ghosting into their body. She tried, but her head wanted to explode. They were just too far away.

The rumbling of the bus grew closer. It was like an earthquake was coming towards Mia, but she didn't stop trying to ghost into that body. She fought against the pain, and reached out to the body that was too far away.

Amir could do nothing but lie on the floor of the bus, bleeding to death. He fought to stay awake, wishing that he hadn't trusted

Zelda or drunk so much that night. He prayed that Mia would somehow get away, but from the look on Zelda's face, he knew that wasn't going to happen.

Blood seeped from Mia's nose, eyes, and ears, and her body couldn't move. The bus's roar grew louder until that noise was all she heard. She felt the bus getting closer, and while she could grab onto the person, they just kept slipping away. It was like catching sand and each grain slipped through her fingers, but little by little Mia held onto more of it.

The bus bore down on her and she realized her time had run out.

Zelda peered out the back window, staring at Mia's body. There was no doubt in Zelda's mind that Mia was alive. She was a strong woman. As the bus ran over Mia, her life in that body was no more.

Amir cried out in anguish, feeling that thump. He sobbed before finally giving into the quiet of possible oblivion.

"Stop," Zelda said. She stared at Amir, knowing that he was the only safe place Mia had to hide in. Fingering her gun and aiming it at Amir, Zelda thought about killing him, ending it right then. But Zelda also knew how much Mia had loved the man. She might not have risked hiding in him. Amir was a good man, and Zelda did like him. There were ways to find out if Mia was in there, and if she was, well, she would cross that bridge when she came to it. Ghosts were hard to track and kill, but no one ever escaped Zelda.

Zelda lowered her gun and put it away. "I must be getting sentimental in my old age." She pulled out her phone. It was going to be a long night for the cleanup crew, but that wasn't in her job description. She only made the messes. Other people cleaned them up.

# CHAPTER 8

**Fifteen years later...**

**Amir winced** as he put on his black suit jacket. The suit was overly tight, or maybe he had just gained a few too many pounds. He couldn't tell if it was the restricting suit, the old bullet wounds, or the frigid cold, but his body was physically reminding him of what had happened on that fateful day.

His wife, Ksenia, watched him as she did every year. Only once had she asked him where he went. He never told her, but she trusted him enough to never ask again.

"Come here," Ksenia said, standing. She was a tall woman, almost reaching Amir's height. She straightened his tie and smiled. "There. Now you look handsome."

"Thank you," he said, smiling back. "You know how I hate ties."

"And they hate you too."

As Amir gazed into Ksenia's dark blue eyes, he realized he was lucky to have found her. The question he hadn't had the courage to ask all these years came from his mouth. "Would you like to come with me?"

Ksenia had to strain her ears to hear her husband's quiet voice. When she realized what he'd said, she gasped. "Are you sure?" She wanted to go more than anything, but she didn't want to force her way into his private moment.

He nodded, still not meeting her eyes.

"Great, but what do I wear? Do you have time to wait while I get dressed? I promise I won't take long."

"What you're wearing is fine."

Ksenia wore jeans and a t-shirt. She knew it wasn't fine. But from the look in his eyes, she knew she might lose her chance at going with him if she gave him time to change his mind. "All right. Let me grab my coat."

It had been years since Amir lived in the city. He and Ksenia owned a house in the suburbs. He drove them all the way back into the city, and they rode in silence. Ksenia was content with that. She knew that Amir would speak when he was ready. Him bringing her along was already more than she ever dared hope. Amir parked in a garage and then they walked to a bus stop. When they eventually boarded the bus, Ksenia noticed that as Amir gripped the bus's bars, his hands were shaky, and he breathed heavily.

Ksenia put a hand on his back. He gave her a small smile before continuing to walk. They sat down and as the bus drove, Amir had a vacant look on his face while he stared out the window. Ksenia watched the buildings disappear and be replaced by trees, as they reached the edge of the city. She opened her mouth to question Amir, but when she saw his thoughtful face, decided against it. It was enough that he trusted her enough to bring her with him. While he never told her where he went and while she never followed him, she knew it must have to do with the day he had been shot and lost his former love, Mia. When Ksenia placed her hand on his, Amir seemed to remember she was there. He squeezed her hand and smiled.

Amir pulled the cord for the bus to stop. Their ride had ended in front of the cemetery. There was a booth selling flowers nearby, and Amir bought orchids. They walked all the way to the back of the cemetery, where Mia's grave lay underneath a tree. Amir pulled a handkerchief out of his coat and cleaned the gravestone before setting the orchids on it.

"Orchids were her favorite," Amir said, never taking his eyes off the gravestone.

"I'm so sorry," Ksenia said, wanting to step forward and comfort her husband, but holding herself back. "I knew she had died, but I didn't know you came here every year."

"That's because I never told you. She died on this day, but there's…more to it than that. You may not believe what I have to tell you."

"You can trust me."

"I know. It's why I married you, and why I brought you here." Amir paused. "What I'm about to tell you is true. It's going to sound outlandish and crazy, but I swear to you by Allah, it's all true. Every word of it."

Ksenia placed a soft hand on his shoulder, waiting for him to begin.

Amir told his and Mia's story—all of it—to Ksenia. He didn't hide anything, lie, or leave anything out. Years ago, before they got married, Amir had thought about telling her, but he was terrified of losing her. It was wrong of him, he knew, but he had already lost one person he loved, and it had devastated him. Yet even though Amir told his wife all the things he and Mia had been through and what she could do, he didn't dare look at her. In a way, it was like he was talking to both Ksenia and Mia.

Once Amir was finished, he dropped to his knees, his face in his hands, shoulders shaking with silent sobs. This was the first time since Mia's death that Amir had allowed himself to grieve like this. The weight of guilt he had carried all these years eased off. When he calmed down, he found his wife kneeling next to him. He finally allowed himself to look at her beautiful face, and when he saw her kind and understanding eyes, it nearly broke him.

He tried to clean up his tear-streaked face. "I'm sorry. I must look a mess."

"It's all right. I don't mind." She reached out and wiped away his tears. "Don't be too hard on yourself. Mia wouldn't want that, and I'm sure she'd forgive you for what happened with that agent."

Amir sniffled. "You believe me?"

Ksenia couldn't conceal a smile. "I don't know if I believe this ghosting thing you say she could do. I do believe that you two loved each other very much, and that her death was tragic. I had always wondered if it was another woman you went off to see each year. Now that I know, I'm not the least bit jealous."

"I wish I could have told her how sorry I was. Over the last fifteen years, it's the one thing I've regretted the most. Her death was my fault."

Before Ksenia could respond, a younger woman's voice yelled, "Hey!" As she ran up the small hill towards them, Amir and Ksenia stood up. The woman was breathing heavily and held crushed daisies in her hand. A streak of red trailed down her long blonde hair. "Sorry I'm late. The holidays can get pretty busy." Her eyes focused on Ksenia. "Who's this?"

"Ali," Amir said. "This is my wife, Ksenia."

Ali's eyes widened. "You finally told her?"

He nodded. "Everything." He turned to Ksenia. "This is the little girl who was once our neighbor." He smiled with pride. "She's all grown up now. Years ago, I told her about Mia's…abilities, and she's come here ever since."

The way he paused made Ksenia wonder if Amir had also told Ali that Mia was responsible for Kate's death. But she didn't push the issue—if Ali didn't know, it wasn't Ksenia's place to tell her.

Ali smiled. "For years, I've been telling him to tell you. It's nice to finally meet you, Ksenia." Ali hugged Ksenia. "Amir's told me about you over the years. I've wanted to meet you for a while now. I'm glad I now have."

Amir fidgeted and scratched the back of his neck. "That's my fault. I should have invited you to our wedding, at least. Free for dinner tonight?"

Ali's eyes lit up and she grinned. "Of course. I've missed your dinners." She looked to Ksenia. "The man you married should have been a world-class chef or at least opened up his own restaurant, instead of being a teacher, as I'm sure you know."

Ksenia leaned into Amir. "I know. Unfortunately, I will be making dinner tonight, and I'm not as gifted as he is."

Ali failed to hide her disappointment. "That's all right. I'd love to come anyway." A huge smile crossed her face. "I want to get to know the woman who filled Amir's heart."

"And I'd love to get to know you as well."

"Great," Amir said. "We'll see you later tonight."

Everyone hugged each other good-bye. Ali went to kneel in front of Mia's grave, but Amir stopped and said one last thing.

"Ali," he said.

"Yeah?"

"I don't think I need to come back here anymore."

Ali nodded. "I understand."

Amir took Ksenia's hand and they walked out of the cemetery together.

As they rode the bus back into the city, Amir felt freer than he had in years. Ksenia was the reason he'd gotten out of the deep depression he was in after Mia's death, but every day he still felt responsible for what had happened to Mia. There was a time when he thought Mia might be hiding in Ksenia especially in the beginning of their relationship. But throughout all the years, she'd never once given him any indication of that. He knew it was wrong of him to think that way, and eventually wrote it off as the burden of guilt he carried.

His loves did have a few things in common, like favorite foods, movies, and even TV shows, but there were far more differences. Ksenia could cook, she taught, and there were even one or two political shows they watched together. Amir eventually dismissed all their similarities as the remnants of his love for Mia, and soon began to love Ksenia in her own right. Yet every so often he thought of Mia, like he was right now.

The way Ksenia leaned into Amir on their bus ride home reminded him of Mia. She was taller and slimmer than Mia, so she didn't quite fit right, but the way she inclined towards him...he just couldn't shake that feeling. It was ridiculous, and he knew that as much as he loved Ksenia, he would never stop comparing them.

When they got home, Amir took off his tie and jacket and breathed easier. "I'm going to go wash up and take a shower."

Ksenia rolled her eyes and sighed heavily. "And I guess I'll get dinner started."

He reeled her in by the waist and kissed her. "Thank you. I'm a lucky man. I love you."

She kissed him back and grinned. "I know. Now hurry up. I've got a dinner to prepare and then I have to get ready for Ali, and for when the little terror comes home." She pushed him away.

He stumbled and laughed before heading up stairs.

Ksenia watched him, then headed into the kitchen. As she prepared their food, she couldn't remember a time when she had been so happy. It was the happiest time in her life, and none of it would have happened had she not ghosted into a body before that bus ran over her.

Mia sighed, remembering that awful day. She had been so fearful that she wasn't going to make it, but she did. Afterwards, she kept ghosting from body to body, unsure of what to do. As much as she wanted to, she didn't control the bodies, instead being content to ride in them like a passenger. The worst part of all was that she had no idea what had happened to Amir. She thought about checking the hospital or going back to their place, but she had a feeling Zelda and her agents were keeping an eye on those places, watching Amir. If they could stop her from ghosting into them and knock her out with gas, she had no idea what else they could do. And most importantly of all, Mia didn't want to put Amir in harm's way again.

For a time, Mia tried to track down Zelda and whatever organization she worked for, to get revenge. She no longer felt the need to be a hero. All Mia wanted was a life where she and Amir could live in peace—together. But every trail of crumbs she followed evaporated.

As time passed, she gave up and focused on getting back together with Amir. That was even more difficult than finding Zelda.

Mia began to watch Amir, and it disheartened her to see what a sad state he was in. She ached to run up to him and tell him she was still alive and that she forgave him, but she didn't. Eventually, he got a teaching job out of the city, thinking that a change of scenery would cheer him up. At that point, Mia thought of a plan to permanently inhabit a body. Luckily, Ksenia worked at the same school as Amir, and she was attractive in a librarian sort of way. While Mia wasn't a teacher, she had learned a lot from Amir over their time together.

Mia had hidden in Ksenia's body at first, learning all the things she could like her passwords, pin numbers, friends, family, hobbies, and—well, everything. During summer break, Mia made a fateful decision and decided to take over Ksenia's body permanently. There was a brief moment when Mia had felt guilt over it, but if there was one thing she had learned from James Calvin,

Zelda, and the others, it was that it was a cruel world out there. There were predators and prey, and after Mia died and lost her body, she vowed never to be prey again.

Mia had molded Ksenia's life into one she would like. The first thing she did was get her hair styled and ditch the oversized glasses. Yet even as much time as Mia had spent with Ksenia, there were still a couple of major problems.

Ksenia had a life of her own, with friends and family who would notice that something was different. Years of memories that Mia couldn't access. She lost friends but gained new ones, especially when she took various classes. She learned archery, took boxing, learned to sew and to cook. Mia had to learn new skills; otherwise Amir would suspect something. She still missed her court shows, though.

Mia knew that she wouldn't be able to ghost anymore. If she did, Ksenia would reassert herself. Yet after a month of being in constant, complete control of Ksenia's body, Mia began to have strange cravings. Foods that she didn't like, she began to enjoy. Books with subjects she had no interest in, she read. Mia even became left-handed. That's when she realized that a lot of the tendencies she now had, were once Ksenia's.

Mia experimented and ghosted out of Ksenia's body, trying to let the woman retake control. But Ksenia never returned. The body was now her own. Mia never knew what exactly happened to Ksenia's essence after that, but there was no going back from what she had done. Soul eater would be a more appropriate term than a ghost. Maybe that's why Zelda had wanted her eliminated. People like Mia *were* far too dangerous for the world.

It took almost a year for Mia, as Ksenia, to break down that self-imposed ice barrier Amir had created. But she had eventually gotten through, and she had never been more thankful.

The front door opened and little footsteps ran across to the kitchen. "Mom! Mom! Look at all the comics Tayta got me."

Mia knew to set down the knife fast. Her daughter slammed into her, squeezing her with a hug.

"Ooof," Mia said, hugging her in return. "Little Terror, did you have a good day with your Jaddah?"

"Yes! Can you read these to me tonight?"

Mia smiled. "Of course. Now I want you to clean up your room. We're going to have company tonight. An old friend of...your dad's." Mia ruffled her daughter's hair. "She was a half-pint like you once."

"Okay. Can I show Dad what I got?"

"Yes, but don't forget to do what I said."

"Okay, thanks, bye!" Jessica ran from the room and headed upstairs.

"And no running!" Mia called out after her. "Hi, Ni'mah. Staying for dinner tonight?"

The older woman plopped down on the stool in front of the kitchen counter. "Goodness, no. I'd love to, but Jessica tired me out. I must get home. It's getting late. I understand why you call her Little Terror. That one has a lot of energy. More than I can handle. Next time, Ksenia. I will go tell Amir goodbye."

"Thanks for watching her today," Mia said. "It meant a lot."

Mia couldn't believe how well she and Ni'mah got along now. She accepted Ksenia more than she ever had Mia. She thought it was partly because of Mia's death and how it affected Amir, but when Jessica was born, the old woman completely accepted Ksenia. Funny how kids changed things.

Mia was going to enjoy the time with her family. She knew it might not last and she wanted one more child, and soon. They had been trying. Despite Mia not being in her original body, a part of her worried that Jessica might be able to do what Mia could. She would have to watch her. Mia knew she was effectively immortal. Amir would eventually die, but she was hoping that would be decades from now, after they'd lived a long and happy life together. When that happened,

Mia vowed to find those responsible for her death, and she would make them pay.

# Author's Corner

Email: marcanthonyjohnson@gmail.com

Facebook: http://www.facebook.com/MarcJohnsonAuthor

Goodreads: http://www.goodreads.com/marcjohnson

Twitter: http://www.twitter.com/Hellsfire

Website: http://www.marcanthonyjohnson.com

www.ingramcontent.com/pod-product-compliance
Lightning Source LLC
Chambersburg PA
CBHW021053130626
46552CB00005B/2082